Jayce turned to Abigail fully. "My dad has never remarried, nor does he date. He used to jokingly say that the Morgan men are like pigeons."

"How so?" Abigail asked.

"They mate for life and if one dies the survivor accepts a new mate only slowly. I thought Haley was my life-mate but obviously I was wrong and maybe high school was too soon a time to know when you've found the right person. I don't know."

Abigail gasped and then tried to cover it up with a cough.

"What?" Jayce asked. "You find me ridiculous don't you?"

"No." Abby shook her head vigorously. "It's just that...I don't think I am worthy to fit into the shoes of your Haley. I can't be a perfect girlfriend. I have too much baggage for that. I don't even think I want a relationship."

She looked at him apprehensively. "Why do you even like me?"

"Honestly, I have no idea," Jayce said, frowning. "You are pretty, yes, but so are a dozen other girls out there. I don't know if I can explain it but when I saw you in the restaurant, it was your first day there. I remember thinking how I hadn't seen you before. You smiled at me, remember, as if you were

waiting for me.

A PAST REFRAIN

BRENDA BARRETT

JAMAICA
TREASURES

A PAST REFRAIN
A Jamaica Treasures Book/July 2014

Published by Jamaica Treasures
Kingston, Jamaica

978-976-8247-18-6
Jamaica Treasures Ltd.
P.O. Box 482
Kingston 19
Jamaica W.I.
www.fiwibooks.com

Dear Reader

I loved writing every single story in the New Song Series. Each book has an element of how past decisions, events, and people can affect the present. The stories are set in Montego Bay, Jamaica's second city, and surrounds the lives of the members of the New Song Band. I hope you enjoy reading the series.

Please, enjoy reading …

Yours Sincerely

Brenda Barrett

ALSO BY BRENDA BARRETT

ABOUT THE AUTHOR

Books have always been a big part of life for Jamaican born Brenda Barrett, she reports that she gets withdrawal symptoms if she does not consume at least two books per week. That is all she can manage these days, as her days are filled with writing, a natural progression from her love of reading. Currently, Brenda has several novels on the market, she writes predominantly in the historical fiction, Christian fiction, comedy and romance genres.

Apart from writing fictional books, Brenda writes for her blogs blackhair101.com; where she gives hair care tips and fiwibooks.com, where she shares about her writing life.

You can connect with Brenda online at:
Brenda-Barrett.com
Twitter.com/AuthorWriterBB
Facebook.com/AuthorBrendaBarrett

Chapter One

October 5th

"**H**appy Birthday, Jayce!" His friends slapped him on the back as he entered the warehouse where the band practiced. He had grudgingly allowed them to throw him a party this year. Usually he hated his birthdays and resisted the calls to celebrate it. So many momentous and traumatic things had happened to him on this day that he had grown to be wary of the date.

It started when he was born. His father said a freak lightning storm happened on the night he made his squalling entry into the world. The storm had plunged into darkness the little clinic where his mother had given birth to him, and the nurses had mixed him up with two other babies.

His father had joked that he might not even belong to him. According to his dad, the clinic sent him home with them because he shared the same light complexion as his mother and what looked like a birthmark similar to one his dad had.

It was also October 5th that his mother had packed two bags: a red leather suitcase that was split at the side, little tendrils of furry fiber sticking from it, and a cloth bag with a picture of Mickey Mouse on the side and told him to be good. He remembered the details of the bags with vivid intensity even after all these years because he had been staring at them so hard, not quite understanding why she was packing without him.

She had kissed him on the forehead, looked him in the eyes, and told him she would be back for him later. He never saw her again. He was just eight years old at the time.

It was also on his birthday that Haley Greenwald, the only girl he had ever loved, was born. For years after they had lost touch, his stupid birthday would remind him that Haley was also celebrating somewhere else—probably with someone else.

He breathed in deeply, accepting a cup of green juice from Melody with an absentminded smile, and sank down into his favorite beanbag chair.

He was thankful for this birthday this year more than any other because just five short months ago he almost died. Surviving being shot in the abdomen made him realize his mortality and caused him do some soul-searching.

He realized that he had just been cruising along through his thirty-four years. He hadn't accomplished anything much. He had started working for his father's security company as an IT auditor after graduating from college. He had deliberately done computer security just so that he could work for his father and fill a gap in the ever-expanding field of computer crimes.

He reasoned that that could be counted as an accomplishment since he had significantly expanded that side of the business.

His father's company was successful and highly regarded among local companies, but somehow that fact didn't give him the tingle of accomplishment that it should.

He wasn't sure if that was all he had wanted to do, though. Sometimes he got the urge to be creative not just with electronics but with poetry too. That usually happened when he went for lunch at the Searock Cafe, close to where the office was, and he saw Abigail, his favorite waitress. She had been inspiring him to write poetry.

He had written several odes to her smile so far. He had it bad for her—real bad—adolescent bad. For the past year, he had been interested in her but he had yet to make a move. Maybe now was the time to do it.

He could have died and yet the only thing he knew about the girl he had been dreaming of was that she had a nice smile and a lovely voice when she said, "Good afternoon, Jayce. What do you want for lunch today?" At least he had made sure that she knew his name.

He looked at his friends around him, talking and laughing. They were all coupled up and happy, especially Aaron, who had his hand lovingly wrapped around Alka, who was so heavily pregnant she looked like she would give birth any minute now.

Alka's trifling ex-husband who had ordered him to be shot had washed his hands of the whole matter and was absolved of the crime by the Indian justice system. The thug who had shot him had mysteriously disappeared, though.

He fiddled with his cup and grimaced. He was getting heartily tired of green juices but drinking the juices actually helped him to sleep better at nights. He couldn't understand why that was. He still had nightmares about the day when he was shot. His counselor said his sleep patterns would eventually return to normal and his night terrors would eventually go away.

He closed his eyes and tried not to remember the shooting incident, but of course the memory was imprinted on the back of his eyelids: one minute he was standing in the buffet line at the Peninsula Hotel in Mumbai India at a security conference, looking forward to eating the various pastries spread out on the mile-long table, and the next minute he heard explosions near him. He hadn't even realized that he was the one who had been hit until he heard the screams near him and saw that his white shirt he had put on that morning was spattered with a deep red stain.

He didn't feel the pain immediately; that had come after. He had fainted from the sight of the blood, like a wuss. According to his doctors, he was shot in the side of the abdomen. The bullets, two in total, had passed through the muscles surrounding the abdomen and had not entered the abdominal cavity at all. If they had, he might not have survived shooting. He had lost so much blood that at first they thought his injury was fatal but the bullets had made a clean exit.

The doctors still thought it was a miracle that he survived the shooting, especially since he was shot at point-blank range. Of course it was a miracle. God had spared him for a reason.

It was a wake-up call for him. The buzzing sounds of people talking got louder; he assumed that the crowd had gotten larger. He idly wondered how many persons Melody and Ruby had invited. They had been the ones to insist on throwing the party.

He didn't open his eyes to see. He was not in the mood to talk, which was unusual for him. These days he was getting more introspective and less talkative, as if his recent brush with death had reset his personality.

When he heard Ruby's disapproving voice above him, he closed his eyes even tighter and groaned.

"Jayce Aman Morgan! I planned this party and you are sleeping in the middle of it! How dare you? I demand that you wake up and enjoy yourself! Now, this minute, or my reputation as a party planner will be ruined!"

He opened his eyes a crack and watched as she pouted at him. Her petite body was clothed in a ridiculously bright orange dress, with a squiggly square pattern that was almost dazzling. Standing beside her was her Amazonian friend, Cynth, who was in a more restful shade of gray.

"That's not Jayce," Cynth murmured. "Jayce is fat. This guy is hunky. Introduce us."

Ruby snorted. "Cynth, this is Jayce." She pinched him. "I had the caterer do all your favorite foods. Get up; eat; be merry. It's your birthday—no moping!"

Jayce opened his eyes wider. "Satisfied now? Ever since you had Amber you've become bossier."

Cynth gasped, putting her hand dramatically over her heart. "Oh my. It's him!"

Jayce grinned. He had been getting the same reaction for the last two months. Even at church, people didn't recognize him now. Church sisters who had avoided him before and hadn't cared to give him the time of day were saying hi to him. Even the older ladies waved to him and giggled.

Suddenly he was eligible again in their shallow little worlds. Suddenly he had raised his profile from the fat guy in the New Song band to the *formerly* fat guy of the New Song band. As one church sister had said, "It is as if he is a new band member."

He found it funny and he watched suspiciously as Cynth crept closer to him. "How come I never realized that you were always this hot?"

Jayce grinned. "I don't know. Were you blind?"

"And feisty," Cynth said grinning. "I like it. So how'd you do it?"

Cynth pulled up a chair and pinched him through his black leather jacket. "He even has toned muscles." Her eyes widened appreciatively.

Jayce rubbed the area where she pinched him and looked between her and Ruby. "What's with you two? Pinches hurt."

He moved farther from Cynth, who looked as if she was contemplating pinching him again.

"Just checking if you are real," she purred.

"No," Jayce said, shaking his head. "I am real. You know I got shot, right?"

"Yeees," Cynth said sarcastically. "I am not that out of touch. I sent you a get well card when you were in the hospital."

"Thanks. Melody handled all my correspondence at that time and I haven't gotten around to reading them yet." He smiled apologetically.

"You asked how I lost the weight? Well, I was placed on a liquid diet for the first eight weeks of my recovery. After I was given the go-ahead to be up and about again, I realized that I had lost quite a bit of weight, so I started going to the gym at my workplace to follow through with the weight loss.

I was so overwhelmed by conflicting advice that I got from the other guys that were there on how best to build muscles and look cut that I asked The General to train me."

"Who is The General?" Cynth asked.

"My father." Jayce grinned. "And he is the best at this whole training thing, believe me; he looks really good for his age. Half the guys in the gym stand back and watch him when he deadlifts, and these guys are highly trained security personnel, some of them ex-army."

"Maybe now you can come and work out with us," Aaron said. The group had drifted closer to him and he realized that he was now the center of attention.

"Maybe," Jayce said, "but I am kind of enjoying my time with The General. He is determined that I develop abs of steel and I am determined to look as good as he does. He is twenty-five years older than I am; he shouldn't look so much better. No way should that happen: I have finally developed a vanity streak and I am in competition with my dad."

"Well, well," Cynth declared, "I thought you were cute when you were fat. You have those hooded male model eyes, which are so sexy but even more so now."

"Down girl." Ruby chuckled and slapped Cynth playfully. "Way down, this is Jayce. He is not into blatant flirtations. You would have to be way subtler than that to get him interested."

Jayce nodded gratefully at Ruby; she knew him well—but he gave Cynth an offhand smile.

"Thanks, Cynth." He stood up and flexed his biceps. "I shall go out and flex my muscles and watch the girls swoon in a heap all around Mobay."

Cynth laughed. "Well, good luck with your newfound sexiness. You have my numbers, right? You can call me anytime; I swoon on command."

Jayce looked at her half fearfully and then shook his head; he headed for the food area with Ruby's laughter following him. He wasn't really hungry. Pastries and sweets no longer appealed to him; food for him was no longer an emotional crutch that he used to drown out his feelings about his past with Haley Greenwald.

He didn't want to disappoint Ruby by not eating any of it, so he took small samples of what were once his favorite foods. He was relieved when Melody walked on the stage area and he could put the plate on the side of the table.

"As the official master of ceremonies for this occasion I must say thank you all for coming. This is an especially emotional birthday party for us because Jayce, our Jayce, our friend, pal, and confidant, the man who never fears to tell it like it is, almost died but was spared. The band will serenade him with his favorite song. Then we'll sing him happy birthday and then we'll give him our heart-felt speeches."

Jayce grinned. "Seriously? Heart-felt speeches. You guys are going overboard."

He then turned to the guys who were walking up to the stage. "I thought you guys said that if you heard my favorite song one more time you would just die."

Carson slapped him on the back. "That was idle talk, man. We are so happy that you are alive I think you can play it a couple more hundred times and we will bite our lips and not say a word. We will even perform it for you as many times as you wish."

Jayce grinned, his heart warmed by the sentiments. He knew that his brush with death had been a wake-up call for all of them. He folded his arms, stood on the sidelines with the rest of the crowd, and listened as the band played *Ain't It Enough* by Maxi Priest.

He didn't know why he loved the song so much; maybe when it was released in June 1996 he was living the lyrics with Haley Greenwald. It had stayed a firm favorite of his since then.

The song brought back all of the wasted and pent-up passion he had for Haley. It also reminded him of all of those years he wasted trying to figure out why she left without saying a word to him. As the band sang the song it brought back memories, stinging memories, memories that he had tried hard to squelch but never really accomplished, even after all these years.

He rocked to the song as Carson did a fair imitation of Maxi Priest. Just then, he made up his mind: today was going to be different. He was not going to dwell on the past; instead his mind drifted to Abigail. He wondered what she was doing right now. He had not seen her since his trip to India.

He wondered if she even took note of his absence, or to her was he just a regular face in a sea of customers that patronized the popular restaurant where she worked.

By the time the guys finished the song, he made up his mind that this evening would be the evening to approach her. He felt compelled to find out more about her. It was his birthday; he was single and to be honest, lonely.

He had not really had the inclination to pursue anyone and had not even attempted to have a relationship with anyone since his youth and Haley. He was a definite case of arrested development, partly because when he was overweight he had been rebuffed more times than he could count and he hadn't had the will to put up with the dating ritual with anyone. It had seemed to him like so much of a hassle.

The very thought of it had made him feel tired but now he was feeling confident. He was willing to put himself out there again and do something positive with his life and he was going to start tonight, with Abigail. He had to approach her sometime; tonight was as good a time as any.

*****

The Searock Cafe was deserted when Jayce drove up. He looked at his watch. It was near closing time, nine o'clock; the party had gone on for a while, considering that it had started early in the evening. He slammed his car door and contemplated going inside the dimly lit restaurant.

He could see Abigail inside, wiping down the tables and rocking to the music that was playing on the restaurant speakers. Her long hair was swinging with the motions of her hand.

He wondered how old she was. He had been wondering about that for the past year. She looked to be in her late twenties. He assumed that she was unmarried because he hadn't seen a ring on her finger, but then again, many married women don't wear a ring.

Please God, let her be single. It was a stupid prayer. If she was married, what would God do—immediately make her single? He drummed his fingers on the car and took in a deep breath.

She stayed inside for twenty minutes more. After the lights were turned off in the front part of the restaurant, Abigail exited with two other girls. A taxi drove up as soon as they exited the building and his heart wilted in disappointment.

She was going to go with the taxi. His chance was shot. What did he expect? It was his birthday. Nothing good ever happened on his birthday, anyway. He watched as her two friends waved to her and got in the taxi and she waved back to them, heading briskly to the brightly lit gate.

His heart hammered in his chest. She was going to walk to her place, wherever that was. That meant that he could offer her a ride home. He jumped into his car, pulled out of his parking spot, and headed to the gate. He pulled up beside her and wound down the window.

She looked across at him and scowled fiercely.

"It's only me, Jayce," he said quickly. "The guy who orders baked chicken and rice and peas every day for lunch. Want a lift home?"

She stopped and stared into the car. "Jayce? You look different."

He shrugged. "Long story."

She sighed. "I don't live far from here. It is just a fifteen minute walk."

"Come on," Jayce said, "tonight's my birthday. Come keep me company. I promise I am not a creep. I love God, I go to church regularly, and I am kind to animals and old ladies."

Abigail chuckled. "I can't believe you want me to just take your word for it."

"I work at Owl Securities," Jayce said hurriedly. "I protect people for a living, which makes me practically the best person to take a ride with at this time of the night."

Jayce watched her anxiously as she waged a war within, contemplating whether she should get into the car. Her face was so expressive, and not for the first time he thought how she looked vaguely familiar, with her creamy peanut butter complexion and thick winged brows. Her hair was in one of those sister locks styles: a fine braided look. She had her hair pulled back in a thick ponytail; she dyed the ends a fire engine red color and it was almost to her waist. She wasn't wearing makeup but her skin had a slight glow, which enhanced her flawless skin.

She was pretty and petite and she had him mesmerized. When she placed a hand on the door handle and then pulled it open, he breathed a sigh of relief. He hadn't even realized that he had held it in, waiting for her to make up her mind.

"I live at the Golden Gate Apartments," she said to him after she sat in the car. "Happy birthday."

"Thanks." He nodded. "My birthdays are not usually the heights of happiness. Aren't you wondering why you haven't seen me around the restaurant?"

She shrugged, turning her expressive brown eyes toward him, and once more he felt a pull of familiarity with her when she looked at him.

"Not really. Obviously you were on a diet," she said. "You look slimmer."

Jayce grinned. "Thanks for noticing."

"Hard not to." She grinned. "So how did you spend your birthday?"

"My friends threw me a party," Jayce said. "It was surprisingly good."

She nodded and looked through the window.

He cleared his throat uncomfortably several times, hoping that she would look in his direction and say something. He did not pick her up for them to drive in silence; he wanted to get to know her better. Obviously, with Abigail he would have to do all the talking.

"So," he asked, "do you have a boyfriend, husband or partner?"

She shook her head. "No. None of the above."

"Is it okay if we see each other sometimes? I mean, I only see you at the restaurant and I would like to get to know you better."

"No," Abigail said, glancing at him. They drove under a streetlight and he could see her expression. She looked slightly appalled and fearful, as if he had asked her something more involved. His curiosity was piqued, and so was his disappointment.

"May I ask why?" He reached the entrance to the Golden Gate Apartments. It was a low-income apartment complex with two-story apartments. The wall surrounding the complex had surprisingly good artwork of various beach scenes, though. There was no golden gate in sight and he wondered how it got that name. He drove onto a graveled driveway that snaked around the complex.

The building looked like it was once painted a beige color. Even in the night, he could see that the walls were peeling and the place looked depressed. A few stray dogs were fighting over a garbage bag in the middle of the pathway leading to the apartments, and he slowed down for them to slink away with bits and pieces of garbage hanging from their mouths.

He waited for Abigail to speak but she only mumbled, "Right here. This is my block."

He dutifully stopped and looked at her curiously as she clutched her handbag to her side and sighed. "Look Jayce, it has been a long day. I am tired. I am really hot and bothered right now."

Jayce released the master lock on the car and watched as she opened the door.

"That's it?" he asked. "You are just going to blow me off like that without an explanation? It's because I am fat, isn't it?" he asked, all of his insecurities coming to the fore.

"You are not fat anymore, remember?" Abigail said swiftly. "Besides, you were always handsome, fat or slim. It's not you, it's me."

Jayce nodded. "I see. You know, I was shot the other day. I could have died. That's why you haven't seen me for months. I thought that since God spared my life, maybe it was time for me to do some things that I have always wanted to do. Like ask you out."

Abigail turned around and looked at him swiftly, such stark concern in her eyes it gave him hope this wasn't the look of a woman indifferent to him. He felt ashamed, though, that he had to resort to shamelessly mentioning that he had been shot to gain her sympathy.

"Are you okay now?" she asked breathlessly.

"Yes." Jayce shrugged. "I am fine."

Her shoulders slumped slightly. "I can't date you Jayce. I am sorry."

He watched as she jumped out of the car and walked

toward her apartment door. She opened the door in haste and slammed it closed.

His body jerked with the slam and the anticipation with which he started out the night died like soda fizz.

"Happy birthday to me," he growled, irritated that he had expected a different outcome.

Chapter Two

Abby took the badge from her shirt and placed it on the chipped counter in the bathroom. She looked in the mirror at her face intently. Since the surgery, her scars had healed and were no longer visible but she was still obsessed with her face. She usually wondered if people saw them but her plastic surgeon had done good work—so good, in fact, that she sometimes stared in the mirror at her reflection as one would stare at a stranger.

She was feeling especially disassociated tonight after she had left Jayce in the car looking hurt and downtrodden. She wished she could date him because the instant she had seen him, she had felt a connection. He was pleasant and jovial and handsome and had the most amazing bedroom eyes—it was as if they drew her in. She had responded to the attraction in his eyes but her life was in a flux.

Her life right now was bogged down with baggage; it wouldn't be fair to him to include him in her mess. She was damaged goods, and she was not only thinking about her face. Her past, and the baggage that came with it, were not worth dragging Jayce into. If he knew her story he would run from her, not ask her out.

She had wondered why she hadn't seen him in the last five months and frequently thought about him and was contrarily happy and sad at the same time that he was no longer coming to the Searock café, but she had no idea that it was because he was shot. He could have died.

The thought made her feel squeamish and slightly nauseous. She wouldn't have seen him again. A part of her wanted to think that Jayce would always be around, even if she couldn't be a part of his life.

As usual, whenever she thought of Jayce she had conflicting thoughts. She knew he liked her—who could miss the way his eyes lit up when they saw her or the way he was always making funny quips to get her to smile?

She pulled off her t-shirt and jeans, put them into the hamper in the tiny bathroom and stood under the shower to cool down. The day had been unusually hot and she had been tempted, more than once, to leave the restaurant and apply for a job somewhere else where she wouldn't need to be on her feet all day, but anywhere else would want information about her, like previous jobs and references and all of that. She didn't have any of that to offer, which was why the Searock had been so perfect. The manager, Kevin, had just asked her if she had a food permit. Since she had gotten one in anticipation of getting the job, she answered yes. He had told her the dress code and told her to report to work in the morning. That had been the interview.

She poured body wash on her bathing sponge and gently rubbed the sponge across her scars. She now had only three that were visible. Like Jayce, she had escaped death.

She wondered where he had been shot. She now had an appreciation for life that she didn't have before her traumatic event.

She sighed. People thought that life was unpredictable. It wasn't. Trials were predictable. It was naive to believe that there would be smooth sailing for anyone. Rich, poor, Christian or not, everybody had problems.

She stepped out of the shower and into her cramped bedroom. The space was so tiny that she tried to spend as little time in it as possible. It was a furnished studio apartment, with a little kitchen area, a bedroom/living room combo, and a tiny closet. It was furnished with the basics: a small settee, which was once red velvet but now had many bare spots and was uncomfortable to sit in, a temperamental countertop electric stove and a hip-height fridge which made a loud buzzing sound in the night. It had taken her a few weeks to get used to the buzzing.

"It could be much worse," she said out loud. "Much worse." She lay on the lumpy mattress that had a sink in the middle. She tried to keep to the right side, which was closer to the door and was firmer.

As usual, she had a hard time powering down. The couple next door, to her right, were quarreling, and she heard a crash and then a scream and then silence. The couple to her left was having sex. She heard their headboard rhythmically hitting her side of the wall. She put her pillow over her ears, hoping that they would stop the knocking soon.

A car pulled up outside and the person driving honked the horn. She breathed in and out deeply; she wished she were not on the ground floor with its paper-thin walls. It was noisy and every vehicle that drove up in the night jerked her out of her sleep.

She turned on her fan. Whenever she did that she could

imagine that the low humming sound it made was rain.

Rain—she loved when it rained. The sound effects that the rain made on the rooftop always made her think of her youth, being cocooned inside and safe. She drifted off to sleep while the breeze from the fan wafted over her, taking her to dreamland...

*****

Abigail was walking on the terrace of a luxurious house in Kingston. She could see the city spread out below her from her vantage point in the hills; the sea was a hazy blue in the distance. She sniffed the air, holding her head to the breeze and giggling as her hair, which she had recently cut to her chin, tickled her nose as it flirted with the breeze. She was feeling carefree, happy, and rich. She wished she could see her father's face now. He probably thought she was suffering without him in her life.

She laughed out loud; she had more things than he could dream of in his miserly existence. She could snap her fingers and people came running, catering to her. She wished Oliver would allow her to feature their house in the *Rich and Famous* magazine. She would ship it to her father with a note. *I triumphed. I survived. Did it without you, you sexist pig!*

She laughed. It would totally blow his mind. Maybe he would froth at the mouth for days. Her mother would probably, in that spineless, gentle way of hers, try to calm him down, while secretly looking at the magazine and envying her lifestyle.

Her mother was not as pious as she tried to appear. She would envy her daughter's lifestyle, but envy was a sin so her mother would take her mousy self and pray about it.

She was happy that she escaped their super strict, rule-laden loony bin, but why did she think about them so much if she was so happy? The thought wasn't worth exploring.

"Hon," Oliver called to her. He had on khaki chinos and a white cotton shirt that was opened down to his navel, his protruding belly on display. His sparsely grayed hair was whipping in the wind.

She waved to him. At sixty-six years old, he was forty-two years older than her and looked it. His florid features reflected his party lifestyle.

He had married her on a whim, mainly because she was young and was in the age group he preferred. She had worked in his company as a receptionist for five months before she was recruited as wife number five. All four of his previous wives had developed some flaw or the other the closer they got to forty.

She knew that she had at most ten more years with Oliver before she reached her sell-by date. Unlike the others, who were constantly begging him for money, she had started saving in a secret account the day she married him, three years ago. She thought of that fund as her insurance money. Oliver was generous with his things and credit cards but he was somewhat tightfisted when it came to raw cash. He needed to track everything. So she saved everything she could get her hands on.

"Hon," Oliver gestured for her to come over to him.

She glided toward him, in her floaty, knee length powder blue dress.

Oliver smiled at her lasciviously. "You are a gorgeous woman." He wrapped his arm around her loosely. "I am having some friends over. We'll be entertaining out here. Don't show yourself until they are gone."

She looked at Oliver with curiosity, but she knew better

than to ask him why. She had known for close to a year now that Oliver had a shady life that paralleled his legitimate businesses. She didn't want to ask questions because she didn't want to know.

She nodded and Oliver kissed her on the forehead.

"Tell Hunter to get out here," he said slapping her on the bottom playfully.

She went inside the mansion and headed toward the kitchen where Hunter was hastily preparing drinks.

"Mr. Hillman needs you," she said to Hunter, who was agitatedly walking around the room.

He looked up at her, his eyes slightly red. "Don't come upstairs," he said to her in the most impolite tone of voice she had ever heard from him. Usually when he spoke to her, he tried to be polite.

She inclined her head slightly and shrugged. She had long come to realize that Hunter Saunders had a higher ranking than any wife that was in residence.

He was Oliver's right-hand man in all things business and personal. She had long worked out that he was also Oliver's henchman and chief confidant and looking at him now, with his bulbous nose and big frame and light almost-red skin and squinty pig eyes, he had more than a passing resemblance to Oliver. He could be his son. He was never acknowledged as such so she didn't ask.

She went to her sitting room. It was a floor below the upstairs balcony and her innate curiosity made her open the balcony doors. She grabbed her phone and put it on 'record' too. She didn't have long to wait before Oliver and his friend were in a discussion.

"I need your side of the government to grant permission for the contract," Oliver was saying to a man who laughed heartily.

"The contract is yours for two million dollars. I can arrange it."

"But the last time you arranged it," Oliver said gritting his teeth, "you had the contractor general investigating my company. I don't forget these things, Findlay."

The man laughed. "It was not my fault."

"It was," Oliver said ominously. "I heard that Cartwright got it instead of me. He paid you more."

Findlay sputtered, "I... I... don't know what you are going on about."

"I have a new inside man," Oliver said ominously. "So the way I see it, I don't need you anymore."

"Listen here, Oliver. I have the prime minister's ear. I am too invaluable for you to even think of getting rid of me."

"Kill him," Oliver said.

Abby gasped and turned off the recorder. She ran inside her sitting room, but not before she heard a thud. Her heart was galloping with fear when she headed to the kitchen area for a drink and saw Hunter Saunders with a sheet wrapped around what looked like a body. Blood was seeping through the sheet. Their eyes met and Hunter growled at her, "What are you doing in here?"

Abby looked at the body in his arms and the ever-spreading stream of blood and shook her head. "I came for a drink."

She turned shocked eyes to Oliver, who was walking behind Hunter, a lilt to his step. "Just taking out the garbage, Hon," he said to her winking. "You can't go up to the balcony now. It needs to be cleaned."

He followed Hunter to the car and the next thing she heard was the car door slamming.

*****

Abby jumped up out of her sleep, her heart racing and her hands sweating. Somebody slammed a car door outside and she could hear the car retreating.

She looked at the clock; it was two o'clock in the morning. She sat up in the bed, shivering. At least she got five hours' rest tonight. Usually she got less. It was hot and yet her hands felt clammy.

She sat up and stared at the blank wall in front of her. When would she forget? When would her mind stop looping the same scene? She closed her eyes and tried to think about something soothing. It wasn't working so she grabbed her Bible instead; usually an hour or so of reading it would settle her mind.

Chapter Three

Jayce entered the Owl Security offices with a scowl on his face after a shower downstairs in the gym. The General had him doing kickboxing this morning, though he had been sluggish. He barely made it through the workout. He hadn't slept much the night before either; he kept remembering Abigail's face when she said, "No, I cannot date you Jayce." Somehow, he hadn't expected that reaction. Women were tripping over themselves to date him now that he had slimmed down. He had half-expected her to do the same; how wrong he was. His confidence had been taken down a notch.

"Hey Jayce." The General walked up behind him. He had showered after gym, as well, and had changed into one of his power suits. "I just got a reminder on my phone that it is your birthday."

"It was yesterday," Jayce said, heading to his office.

"Oh," The General said. "I don't know why I always get the dates wrong."

"Because it is the same day that your wife left you," Jayce said mercilessly. He knew The General was not prone to forget anything; he chuckled at The General's grimace. "It is also the same day that bad things happen in our family. Houses burn down, cars get wrecked and freak storms happen."

The General chuckled. "Well it's gone, thankfully, and it's a new day, so happy belated birthday. Did you send me that report from the bank?"

"No," Jayce said grumpily. "I have a million and one technical things to work on. I need a personal assistant. I am going to be out of the office for a while today, too. I am working on a prototype with Xavier."

"Oh yes, the prototype," The General said. "Come join me in my office; let us discuss that."

Jayce followed his father into his office. It was pristine—clean and neat. The General liked order, a trait left over from his army days. On his walls were several plaques that celebrated his various business milestones. He had gotten the Chamber of Commerce Employer of the year award last year, and there were several pictures of him with the country's movers and shakers. Whenever prospective clients came to the office they were usually duly impressed by them. Jayce took a seat and watched as The General pushed his hands into his pockets.

"I know the business is growing by leaps and bounds, thanks in part to you. This new technology that you are working on with your friend Xavier, if it materializes into what you are describing, will be really something else."

Jayce smiled. His father rarely gave him credit for anything but since his near-death experience his dad had been doling out credit and compliments left, right and center.

"You are quite right; you should get a personal secretary.

Make sure she has level two clearance."

Jayce sighed. He was not in the mood to go secretary hunting. That was the main reason he had been putting it off. "I'll ask Simone to do it; she's the HR person."

His father shrugged. "Knowing how picky you are, I thought you would want to choose this person for yourself."

"You are right." Jayce rubbed the back of his neck contemplatively. He knew whom he wanted to be working by his side as his personal assistant. He had one candidate in mind.

He smiled ruefully at his father. "I'll choose my own secretary."

"Good. Can you choose her by next week?" The General said, sitting down and frowning. "You have a whole slew of reports for me."

Jayce got up. "Fine."

He went to his office, past the empty area where a secretary's desk would fit quite nicely, and sat in his chair. His office was nowhere near as neat as his father's. He had banks of monitors and computers and two desks. One of them was piled high with technical paraphernalia. It was a geek heaven, and it was not all for work, either. He had been working with Xavier on several gaming applications for smart phones. He turned on a monitor and put his feet on the desk, leaning back in his chair and staring at the air vents.

He wondered what Abigail was doing now; was she breaking some other dude's heart for breakfast? He remembered how he had reached out to her and she had stopped him in his tracks, saying, "It's not you, Jayce, it's me."

Whenever a person said that it was just a throw-away statement to soothe the other person's ego. Of course it was him. She found something wrong with him. She was just not interested. He could live with that. It was not his first rejection. It's just that this particular rejection hurt. For some strange, unfathomable reason, he was drawn to her like he hadn't been drawn to another woman for more years than he cared to count.

He contemplated asking her to be his secretary. He didn't even care if she didn't have secretarial experience. He just wanted her close to him.

The internal phone rang and he picked it up—he should get into work mode. He glanced at the clock. It was eight o'clock on the dot, and the call was from the front desk.

"Hi Jayce," Cordell, the receptionist, said politely. "A Mr... er...Doctor...Pastor Greenwald is out here to see you."

Jayce swallowed. He was? Why?

"Jayce?" Cordell prompted.

Jayce realized that he had been silent for too long. "Yes." He cleared his throat. "Yes, send him through to my office."

He put down the phone slowly. From the days he used to date Haley, Pastor Greenwald had always made him feel nervous. He had heard that Greenwald had tried to visit him when he was bedridden from that gunshot wound but Melody had managed to hold him off.

He should thank Melody once more for the splendid job she performed as his social secretary, nurse, and general dogsbody. He wondered if she wanted to work as his secretary. He dismissed the thought instantly. She would hate it; she loved being the one in charge and would organize and boss him around in his own office. He wanted someone more pliable or obedient as his secretary.

He smoothed out his shirt and stared at his computer screen, hoping to appear busy. He didn't want the critical eyes of the pastor to find anything wrong with him. Why that should matter now, he wasn't sure, but Pastor Greenwald always had that effect on him.

Pastor Greenwald's perfume preceded him into the room—a strong, overpowering scent, kind of like the man himself. When he appeared at the door, he opened his eyes widely and looked at Jayce.

"You look good," he said in greeting. "Younger. Slimmer."

"Thank you, sir," Jayce said nervously. His last meeting with the man was when he had visited him about the band performing some months ago, and that had been super uncomfortable, with Jayce itching to ask about Haley and the pastor glowering at him as if he had committed some recent sins that he neglected to atone for.

He had managed to avoid him at church ever since that meeting. That wasn't hard to do because Greenwald was in high demand. The church flock loved his heavy-handed fire and brimstone hard-nosed style. As one person said, "The Lord's presence is back in the church." He had asked why she thought it had gone.

Greenwald had a friendlier expression on his face now. He was a big, blustery fellow with dark skin, a thick body, and a booming voice. "I heard you were not having visitors when you were ill. I prayed for you nevertheless."

Jayce nodded. "Thank you. Have a seat." He gestured to one of the three chairs in front of his desk.

Greenwald sat in the middle chair, placed his briefcase on one of the others, and straightened his tie. He was dressed formally. Jayce sat down, facing him.

"So how can I help?" he asked.

Greenwald shook his head. "I am just here to see you as your church pastor. I can never seem to get the chance to see you otherwise. I figured it was the start of the business day and you were at work; you shouldn't be too busy yet."

"Oh," Jayce said. "Thank you for the concern. I am fine now. I have been back at work for two months now."

Greenwald nodded. "It is a miracle that you are alive."

"Yes." Jayce nodded. "It is, and I am grateful."

"You should share your testimony at church," Greenwald said, leaning back in his chair.

"I will," Jayce said. "There is nothing much to tell, though—no grand story. I didn't even know what really happened. I was standing at the food line and then I was shot and then I fainted."

Greenwald half smiled. "The Lord must have spared you for a reason, Jayce. Maybe he is giving you one more chance to make your life right."

Jayce cleared his throat. "There is nothing overly wrong with my life. I am trying to walk the Christian pathway. Like everybody else, I have my struggles."

Greenwald nodded. "So are you in a relationship now?"

"Er..." Jayce felt like fidgeting. Why was Greenwald asking him that? Had he forgotten their history, when he had kicked him out of his house and told him never to contact his daughter again?

"No, not yet," he said, thinking about Abigail. Maybe he would pursue her despite her deep reluctance to have anything to do with him—and then again, maybe not. Maybe he would ask her if she wanted to work for him. He hadn't made up his mind yet.

One thing he knew for sure was that he was not going to let her reject him as she had done last night and just let it slide. He needed to know why she couldn't date him.

Greenwald coughed. "Well, it is not seemly for a Christian man your age to be playing the field."

Jayce laughed. "I am not playing, nor have I ever played, the field."

"Really?" the pastor said. "Remember Haley?"

Jayce grimaced. How could he forget? He didn't think he

would ever forget her. "I loved Haley. I wanted to marry her. She was my only girlfriend. You saw us kissing and like a demented madman, you forced us apart."

"She was too young," Greenwald said, "and that was the right decision."

Jayce sighed. "Where is Haley now?" he asked, a tendril of pain pinching his heart. Despite himself, he still cared about her. She would always be his first love. What he felt for her had been so potent that he still felt vestiges of the emotion whenever he said her name.

"I have no idea," the pastor said uncomfortably. "She left the house when I wasn't there and she has not tried to keep in touch. I say good riddance to her."

"That's cold!" Jayce said. "You don't even know if she's dead or alive."

"She's not dead." Greenwald snorted. "If she were, I would know. One day she'll be back like the prodigal daughter. If she's no longer rebellious and willful we'll welcome her back with open arms."

Jayce winced. He wondered how Pastor Greenwald could so easily write off his own child but as he remembered, Haley had not really liked her parents and their rules much. They had gone overboard in their strict routine with her. He wasn't surprised that she hadn't kept in touch with them.

He had a special appreciation for The General now. As bad as he was and as gruff as his attitude was, Jayce knew that The General would walk through fire before he lost touch with him. The General would rather die than have him out of his life. Of course, The General wouldn't admit that.

He absently answered all of Pastor Greenwald's questions and said goodbye to him inattentively. The pastor's visit disturbed him. It brought to the fore all his past thoughts about Haley.

He looked at the clock again. He had tons of work to do, but for just ten minutes he would indulge himself in walking down memory lane. Maybe then he could shake the feeling of unease that he had gotten after talking about Haley.

September 1994

At Cedar Hill High the school year had just begun and already Jayce and his friends, Aaron, Logan, Carson, and Ian, were sitting under a tree near the tenth grade block. They had spent most of the summer together in their band and now they were back at school. School could not compare to the excitement of the past summer. They had traveled to other parishes and played at concerts, fairs, and fun days. They had been the main band for a series of evangelistic meetings in July.

Jayce had still not adjusted, to the rigidity of the school mode after his summer and he had taken with him a fixation on Beres Hammond, the best singer in the entire world in his humble opinion. He had memorized most of his songs over the last few months, even the old ones like *I'm So in Love,* and he was humming it now.

Carson snickered, "Jayce, when you love something do you have to sing it over and over again? You are killing us with this one."

Jayce grinned. "Hush."

"Well, it would be nice for you to find a girl to sing it to, instead of singing it to us," Logan said.

"I'll do just that, but it won't be easy," Jayce said. He looked over the crowds of students walking toward their classes. There were several girls walking about briskly. He knew most of them. Cedar Hill High was a private church school, and they were the popular New Song band and well-liked by the girls. Even the shy ones made up excuses to talk to them on a regular basis.

He hadn't found any girl that he liked yet. Unlike his friends, who would discuss the virtues of several of the females on the campus, he just didn't find anyone attractive. He was actually wondering if something was wrong with him, developmentally. According to most of the health education classes he had been to, teenage boys his age were supposed to be raging balls of hormones just waiting to pounce on the innocent virtues of any girl.

He certainly didn't like any of the girls he came in contact with—well, maybe at one time he had felt something for Alice Murray but Carson had made it clear to them that Alice was out of bounds to everyone but him. She was the only girl in the band and she only had eyes for Carson, so there wouldn't be any luck there for him, even if he defied Carson and pursued Alice.

He always wondered what that felt like: the infatuation, the breathless anticipation that his friends seemed to have for some girl or the other. He wondered what it would be like for that girl to look back at him adoringly, and what the ritual of cherishing her and being a couple felt.

He was still humming the Beres Hammond song when he saw her; she was walking toward the 9th grade block, a book in her hand and a rucksack over her shoulders.

She wore glasses and her hair was pulled back in a ponytail with a ribbon at the end of her plait. Who wore ribbons anymore in high school? he thought fondly. She looked refreshingly different to him.

"I am going to sing the song to her one day," he said, pointing to her even though she was in the distance.

"Good luck to you and that," Logan snorted. "Her father teaches Biology here. Though I hear that he was a pastor in another parish. I would be afraid of him if I were you. He is built like a tank and when he talks the buildings shake like an earthquake. Besides, she is probably his youngest daughter. I think her name is Haley."

"How old is she?" Jayce asked, not really hearing Logan's warning about her father. He was staring at the girl in wonder. It was as if on seeing her he was thwacked in the chest with a fist.

"I don't know," Logan said. "Go ask her, or you could ask her what she's reading, start a conversation. I must warn you, that's my pick-up line."

The other guys laughed when Jayce got up. "I used to think your pick-up line was corny but not today." He straightened his spine and walked over to where she was standing.

She had stopped in front of the library. She pushed her glasses, which were a shade too big for her, up her nose and stopped him when he approached.

"Excuse me," she said. Her lips were the deepest shade of red, almost bordering on black. "Can you help me please, where is 9A?"

Jayce was pondering if she had on lipstick. He was staring at her so fixedly that he barely heard the question.

She looked like a cute nerd who was wearing makeup; her skin was that smooth and perfect.

"You have to tell me your name first…how old you are, and you have to have lunch with me."

She gasped and clutched her book to her chest. He expected her to storm off. He looked back at the guys and they were watching him intently. He tensed himself for the guffaws that would follow when she walked off but instead she said primly, "The name is Haley. I am fourteen, and of course I will not have lunch with you. I don't know who you are."

Jayce grinned. "Jayce Morgan, I am sixteen and in final

year. Is that too old for you?"

"You are not too old, just too bold for me," Haley said, grinning. "Besides, I can't be seen with boys. My father thinks all boys are up to no good. Where is 9A?"

Jayce chuckled. "Your father sounds ominous. I hope I don't have him for Bio class."

"Me too." Haley grinned. "It's bad enough to have to endure him at home."

She moved away and then turned back. "Where do you normally have lunch?"

"At the cafeteria," Jayce said readily.

"Well, I could sit near to you at lunch time," Haley said, shrugging. "See you then."

He walked her to her class, and by the time she turned inside and waved to him he knew that he had found her, the girl that would inspire him to be a teenage boy with raging hormones.

Chapter Four

Jayce was jerked out of his reminiscing by a telephone ring. He answered it almost reluctantly, so engrossed was he in his memories.

"We have to meet now," Xavier said excitedly. "I think I made a breakthrough."

Jayce whistled. "But we just started working on the prototype. You are a genius."

Xavier chuckled. "Not really. I have a lot of downtime these days, and since Ian finished the house, I was thinking of incorporating some of the security features that you had proposed in the concept. Want to come up to my place? You haven't been there since the housewarming."

"No," Jayce said, "let's have a lunch meeting close to the office, instead; your place is too far away. I have gazillion things to do this morning. Want to meet at the Searock Cafe?"

"Sure," Xavier said, "prepare to be amazed."

"I know I will be," Jayce said.

He hung up the phone and turned on his monitor. He was looking forward to going to the Searock Cafe for no other reason than that he would see Abigail.

He sighed. It felt as if his life was mirroring his past. Haley had inspired his teenage heart with longing, and now Abigail was doing the same thing to him as an adult.

*****

The Searock Cafe was just a four-minute drive from the office. In fact, he could have walked it and he would have if the day hadn't looked so overcast. The air felt still and heavy, as if there was going to be a serious downpour later on. Even the sea, which was a yard away from the cafe, looked calm— too calm, like it was preparing for some mischief later in the day.

Jayce glanced in his rearview mirror. He had still not gotten used to his new physique. His gigantic belly was gone and in its place was the beginning of a six-pack. His face was now chiseled, almost like The General's. If he hadn't inherited his mother's light complexion, he could have passed as a younger looking version of his very muscular father.

He had never seen himself like this before. In high school, he had been skinny. He had gradually packed on the pounds during college, but now he looked just right. Well not quite. He still had a way to go; he wanted to look as fit as The General.

He straightened up from the mirror, not wanting to appear vain, and looked across at the cafe; as usual, the lunch crowd was swarming the place.

The Searock was one of those places where the food tasted good and the prices were super-reasonable. He headed to the VIP area, which was upstairs in the air-conditioned section of the restaurant. He could discuss the new prototype with Xavier without the distraction of the downstairs buzz and he could also get to observe Abigail without the usual mad rush. He hoped she would be working in the VIP section.

Xavier was already ensconced in the far corner of the restaurant when he entered. He was engrossed with something on his computer screen.

"What's up?" Jayce asked, looking around for Abigail. He sat down, disappointed that she wasn't up there. He saw another waitress, Rachel, working.

He frowned, trying to concentrate on what Xavier was telling him, but he knew the instant she came into the room. All the hairs on the back of his neck stood at attention. He watched as she looked around with a notepad in her hand. She made eye contact with him and then inhaled deeply.

So she isn't uninterested in me then, he thought gleefully. Her body language screamed that she was tense.

She walked over to them slowly. Today she was wearing the requisite white t-shirt and blue jeans but she had on a colorful red bandana that tied back her long hair and exposed her high cheekbones.

"What can I get you folks today?" she asked, her voice husky.

Xavier's head snapped up from the computer and he stared at her with a frown. He looked across at Jayce's dreamy, spaced-out look and pushed him.

"Uh," Jayce cleared his throat. "Have you always wanted to be a waitress?"

Abigail raised her eyebrows. "That's not on the menu."

"I know," Jayce shrugged. "I just wondered, you know, if you would like to do something else."

Abigail stood with the notepad awkwardly. She had come in late today. She had overslept and was feeling sluggish.

The restaurant manager, Kirk, warned her that if it happened again she would be fired.

One infraction and he was ready to kick her out. *Easy hire, easy fire*, she had thought snidely. Not for the first time she wished that she had a different job. The pittance that she made as a waitress was not going to help her on her quest to be independent again, and here was Jayce asking her if she wanted to do something else.

She cautiously answered, "Sure I would. Now can I take your order?"

Jayce smiled. "I am looking for a secretary. Have you ever done any secretarial work?"

Abigail nodded slowly. "As a matter of fact I have."

Jayce took out a business card from his shirt pocket. "If you are interested in working for me, give me a call. You have to call before next week, though. I have a deadline to fill the position."

She reluctantly took the card and pushed it into her jeans pocket. She shouldn't even be entertaining working for anybody who would want to know her work history.

When Jayce and Xavier gave her their orders and she walked away, Jayce watched her round, perfect, pert bottom and swaying hips. "I like her."

"I can see that," Xavier said mockingly. "She seems familiar."

"How?" Jayce asked.

"I don't know," Xavier said. "Maybe I met her some place before or saw her on television."

"On a model show?" Jayce asked, chuckling.

"I don't know; can't recall watching any of those but yes, she is pretty," Xavier said, pointing to the monitor. "Let's take a look at this again. I guess after we sort this out I will be a more reasonable man to live with. Farrah claims I have gone manic."

Jayce chuckled. "How is Farrah these days?"

"She's stressing me out for a baby, because she wants our kid to be in the same age group as Alka, Alice and Ruby's. She has this grand plan that the New Song band could be extended to the next generation, with all of our children forming another band."

Jayce grinned. "That actually sounds like a good plan, and you don't seem stressed out."

Xavier smiled. "I am not really, it's just that I wouldn't mind having one more year with just us. No babies."

"Ah, how sweet," Jayce said. "Do you realize that out of all of us guys, I am the only unmarried, lonely one? The only single, pathetic one."

Jayce cupped his chin. "Am I being punished for something? I mean, I am thirty-four. I am finally in shape. I sing in a band; I play the guitar and piano and drums. I am the only one of the six of us guys who can play all instruments, and I write poems. I am creative and sensitive. I earn a decent living working in a successful company."

Xavier chuckled. "You really sound good. It's a pity you are the one who is saying it and not that waitress."

"Abigail, her name is Abigail," Jayce cleared his throat. "I asked her out. Maybe I wasn't as polished as I could have been, so she turned me down."

"She likes you," Xavier said.

"You think so?" Jayce asked excitedly. "How can you tell?"

Xavier scratched his chin. "Let's see. There are certain nonverbal gestures that gave her away the minute she stood here, like her eyes kept straying to you and she gazed at you with a hunger that was palpable, like she wanted to touch you and was restraining herself."

"She did?" Jayce growled, "Are you playing with me?"

"Nope," Xavier said, his face was serious. "I was shocked at the wealth of feeling firing from her eyes."

Jayce smiled. "You are actually saying this with a straight face?"

Xavier nodded. "Of course. Now it's up to you to leverage this information and pursue her with the kind of single-minded determination you pursued Haley in the past. Remember how you used to write her poems and have us put music to them? Boy, you were sappy."

Jayce sighed. "I thought about her today."

Xavier quirked his brow. "Really? You still think of Haley Greenwald? Forget I said that. I was still thinking about Farrah when I left Jamaica. For me it was almost every day, until gradually it became less intense. I wonder where Haley is now..."

He stopped speaking as Abigail approached. She had a tray in her hand and she deftly took off the food.

"Bon appetit," she said cheerfully.

"Thanks," Jayce said. Before she could turn away, he asked impulsively, "Have supper with me this evening. I'll pick you up here after work."

She spun around, her mouth opened slightly. "Jayce..."

"You can't embarrass him in front of company," Xavier said quickly. "It would crush his spirit. The guy almost died; cut him some slack."

Abigail looked at him so long that Jayce almost wanted to squirm.

"Okay," she finally said. "I get off at six tonight."

Jayce nodded jerkily, trying to look casual, but inside he was singing.

Xavier closed the laptop. "I will take this up with you tomorrow. I have a feeling that you will be useless after this."

Jayce was still staring at the space that Abigail had occupied with a look of astonishment on his face.

"Did you hear that, Xavier?" he asked, whispering.

"Yes," Xavier chuckled. "The girl said yes. Supper, though? Who asks a girl for supper? You sound thoroughly old fashioned; the miracle is that she doesn't seem to mind it."

Chapter Five

"So here we are," Jayce said, feeling a little bit awkward since Abigail entered the car. He had picked her up after the restaurant closed and had driven to his house. He couldn't think of anywhere else to go, and he had asked her to supper. He figured that a restaurant was out of the question because after spending all day in one it would just feel like an extension of her job.

His unpainted house loomed in the car lights. He had bought the house on a whim two months ago. It was on the same street as Logan and Melody's and had been a fixer-upper. He had thought that he could help with the renovations but his contractor had told him bluntly that he was in the way. It was recently finished; the men had not yet removed the debris from the front of the large lot, nor had they finished painting the outside of the place.

"Is this where you live?" Abby asked him. "I must confess I saw you as more of an apartment dweller, with a cat."

Jayce got out of the car and opened her door. "I lived in an apartment but after I got shot I stayed with my friends Melody and Logan and the owner of this house was selling, so one morning while walking by I had an epiphany: why not live in a house and plant a garden? I'll get a cat eventually. How'd you know I was a cat person?"

Abigail cleared her throat. "I didn't. This is a nice neighborhood, and the house is gorgeous. Wow."

"Thanks," Jayce said ruefully. "I hounded my friend, Ian, to design it for me, or should I say redesign and update it? As usual he did an excellent job."

He opened the heavy front door. "Sorry about the echo. I have not gotten around to buying furniture and all of those homely things. It was just recently finished. I started living here just two weeks ago, actually."

Abigail was looking around. "It's really nice. I love these ceilings…gives the place a cathedral-like air."

Jayce looked pleased. "It has four bedrooms and an equal amount of bathrooms. I even have a pool. It's not yet filled with water, though. Maybe when it is full you can come over and have a swim?"

Abigail swung around and looked at him. "Jayce…"

"Moving too fast?" he asked contritely. "Sorry." He headed for the kitchen. "This is the only place in the house that is thoroughly furnished and finished. No paint fumes either."

She followed behind him slowly. "I like the forest green accents. You even have a forest green kettle. That's a lovely color."

Jayce frowned. "I don't think I consciously chose the color. This might sound odd but I had a girlfriend once that loved the color and since then I have loved it too."

Abigail stilled. "Really? What's her name, this girlfriend?"

Jayce grinned slightly. "No, no, no," he shook his head, "I

am not going to be that guy. The one that talks about another woman while he is with somebody else."

He grimaced, "I learned my lesson a long time ago—that is bad dating etiquette."

Abigail smiled. "So is this a date?"

"Well..." Jayce scratched his chin. "Is it?"

Abigail drummed her fingers on the granite counter top. "I was thinking it was more of a casual interview. I thought about what you said today and I would really like a change of jobs."

Jayce felt disappointed. He had wanted her to be here because she wanted to hang out with him and get to know him better but then again, working with her every day would be advantageous to him. He would definitely get to know her better.

He opened the fridge. "What would you like to eat? I make the best sandwiches."

Abby shook her head. "I am not in the mood for sandwiches, I feel like having some cornmeal porridge like my grandma used to make it, with lots of cinnamon and pimento leaf..." She licked her lips.

"I can do that." Jayce stared at her moist, dark pink lips and then grinned at her. "I haven't had that in ages...since high school, actually. I never really had the taste for it after..."

He looked at her with a bemused expression on his face. "You know, when my ex-girlfriend, no...sorry," he stuttered. "Forget it."

Abby was staring at him, transfixed, as if she was waiting to hear what he had to say. She broke the tension by looking away to a big black and white picture that he had taken with the band from high school days.

"So that's your band?" She pointed to the picture.

"Yup," Jayce said, gathering the fixings for the porridge.

"We were so young and idealistic then. That picture was taken after a church concert. We were fund raising for something or the other."

Abby got up and moved closer to the picture and whispered, "1995."

When he turned around, he saw her touching it almost reverently.

"How'd you guess that?" Jayce came over to stand beside her. He was so much taller than her that her head reached him at his chin. She could smell his cologne. She inhaled and closed her eyes. He smelled just right, musky and slightly minty.

"Seriously," Jayce said over her head, squinting at the picture to see if a date was on it.

Abby snapped out of her dazed inhalation and shrugged. "Lucky guess?"

She moved away from him and tried to avoid his eyes.

Jayce inclined his head to one side and then frowned. "Tell me about you, Abby. Where are you from? Where have you worked before? Where did you go to school?"

Abby sat down on the stool and sighed. "So the interview has started?"

Jayce went over to the stove and started stirring the pot. "Yes, if you want to call it that. You have really piqued my curiosity."

Abby stared at her reflection in the countertop. "I was born on February 1. My parents are dead to me. I am an orphan, no near family members to speak of. I am from Kingston. I have worked in companies before and I have done secretarial work."

"School?" she heard Jayce ask above her and she jerked up and looked at him guiltily. "I work in security," Jayce said gently. "I know when someone is lying. You are not very good at it."

She closed her eyes. "I can't tell you about my past, Jayce. I can't tell anyone."

Jayce stared at her for the longest while. "If you want to work for me, you have to get a level two clearance. There is a thorough background check done on you by our company. It is standard company policy; we deal with sensitive information for some large companies, so we usually check if you have loans, a criminal record, unpaid bills—that sort of thing."

Abby swallowed. "I don't have any of those things but how can you find out all of that?"

"Easy," Jayce grinned. "My dad has contacts that even law enforcement doesn't have access to. With technology the world is much smaller than you think."

"So if level two is so intense, what does level three clearance entail?" Abby asked hoarsely.

Jayce turned off the stove. "Level three is deeply personal. We check out even your close family—that kind of thing. Fact is, some companies request us to do that for them, especially before hiring top executives."

He shrugged. "We'd check if you have lovers, how many, a drug habit, mental issues, what you say on the Internet—the whole gamut. Privacy is just a by-word these days. That's why it's always best to be honest in your dealings—saves a lot of time and energy."

Abby gasped. "Wow."

"Yes, wow." Jayce grinned. "This is where you volunteer to tell me all."

Abby drummed her fingers on the table, only breathing a sigh of relief when Jayce turned back to the stove. She couldn't stand his intense scrutiny.

*****

After Jayce laid out bamboo placemats around the nook and they were eating, Abby said tentatively, "This is good."

Jayce nodded. "It is. I am surprised that I actually remember how to cook it. This is comfort food. Only thing missing is the rain."

Abigail grinned. "Yup, and raisins. Do you have any?"

Jayce held his spoon midway. "You eat raisins with your porridge too?"

"Yes," Abigail said, and then hastily added, "but if you don't have any, that's fine. I mean, it's not like I eat raisins with my porridge all the time; lots of people do it...why on earth do you look so shocked?"

Jayce looked at her contemplatively. "I have raisins." He got up, got a box from the fridge, and handed it to her.

"I am not shocked. I am sorry for acting so strange," he said heavily. "I had a girlfriend in high school, the same one I have been trying to avoid talking about...I know it's long ago and this is going to sound funny, but you are the only woman I have really liked since then and she liked raisins in her porridge too. It's like a sign."

"You haven't liked anyone since high school?" Abigail looked at him skeptically. "Are you serious?"

She poured out the raisins on top of the porridge and Jayce watched as she scooped a spoonful into her mouth. The seemingly innocent gesture was alarmingly a turn on.

He scrambled to speak. "Yes. Well, technically I was in college. Unfortunately, I am severely picky where women are concerned. I candidly confess that I actually thought I was asexual or something until I met Haley when I was sixteen...and now there's you."

He laughed deprecatingly, "I actually went to the doctor

for it. I thought I had some kind of condition. My friends tried to set me up but I am so picky that I frustrated them. Once or twice, I have made an effort to see a few ladies in my church, you know, but there is always something with them. Last person was Leona," he shuddered. "She used to cook elaborate meals for me; that was a turn-off."

Abigail gazed at him with her mouth slightly opened.

"I know. I know, it sounds absurd," Jayce said. "The doctor referred me to a psychiatrist. The psychiatrist said that I am severely distrustful toward women and that could be coloring my views in any new relationships. The thing is, I haven't been motivated to have any relationships, so really I couldn't be distrustful toward women as he said. I hope I am not making you uncomfortable?"

Abigail cleared her throat. "No. No. I just...I have never met a guy like you before. You have only had one girlfriend since high school. And you are what age now, thirty-something?"

"Thirty-four, my birthday was yesterday," Jayce said uneasily. "How old are you?"

Abigail toyed with her spoon. "Don't you know you shouldn't ask a girl her age just like that? You should wait until the second date."

Jayce laughed, "Really? Let me guess then—twenty-six."

Abigail grinned. "That's flattering."

"I'll have to know if you are to come and work for me," Jayce said, pushing away his bowl. "It would be on your resume."

Abigail looked at him keenly. "So I guess that's it then. I can get the job?"

"I could convince my father not to investigate your background. I could vouch for you, but he might not say yes since he trusts no one," Jayce offered. "In the meantime, you can tell me your secret. Be honest with me."

"I am..." Abby inhaled and pushed her half-empty bowl away. It made a clink as it touched Jayce's.

" I...ah..." A look of pleading filled her eyes. "Please, Jayce, I can't really say why I..."

Jayce watched as she muddled her way through the speech and then abruptly stopped talking.

"Did you commit a crime?" he asked gently. That was the worst thing he could think of. He could not hire her if she had a record, not as a secretary with access to all sorts of information.

She looked at him shocked. "No!"

"Okay, okay," he said relieved. "You can tell me in your own time."

He never trusted people like this—it was a leftover from the day his mother had looked him in the eyes and told him that she would be back for him but never returned. However, here he was, taking Abigail's word that she wasn't a criminal. Her vehement no, and the earnestness in her eyes did it for him.

Her past was so bad she couldn't tell him and like a besotted fool he didn't care. He wanted her to work with him. He wanted to see her every day. He wanted to smell her subtle perfume and watch as her brown eyes lightened up with laughter or turned liquid with soulful pleading.

He was a goner. The General would castigate him for this in the future, he was sure of it, but he was going to hire Abigail. He suddenly realized that he didn't know her last name.

What's your surname? he asked, aghast at his own omission.

"Petri," Abigail answered slowly. "Does this mean that I can get the job?"

Jayce nodded. "I'll need your resume. I can't bypass that."

Abigail nodded.

"Be honest on it; do not falsify important details," Jayce said, a warning tone in his voice.

"I will." Abigail nodded vigorously. "Definitely."

Chapter Six

Two weeks later Jayce was not so sure that hiring Abby was the best thing. She was extremely efficient, impressing even his father, but she was keeping him even further away than she did when she worked at the restaurant. He would crack a joke and she would laugh politely. He would ask her out but she would take her lunch or dinner or whatever she had to eat and then she would turn her pretty doe eyes on him and affect sorrow that she couldn't eat with him.

It was depressing. He threw a crumpled piece of paper in the bin, closed his eyes with a heavy sigh, and leaned back in his chair.

"Jayce," Abby said breathily somewhere near him. He heard her heels clicking on the floor, heading toward him, but he stubbornly refused to open his eyes to look at her. Her image was burned on his eyelids anyway.

She had made the absurd decision to wear pink today. Absurd, because pink highlighted her dusky brown skin and gave her a healthy glow. He had had his fill of staring at her this morning. She was in a rose pink blouse that molded her slim curves and a pencil skirt that fell a little below her knees, and she had a pink band holding her long hair together in a curly ponytail. She looked like a model trying to be a secretary or a dream giving him nightmares.

"Jayce," Abigail said again, insistently. "Are you okay?"

He grunted. "Yes, sure."

"The landscaper called. He said you have an appointment with him at the house."

Jayce cracked an eye open and she came into his field of vision. Dark red lips—he wondered what it was about women with naturally deep red lips that made him so fascinated. She licked hers and he watched the action as if it were in slow motion.

"Jayce!" Abigail said, leaning on the desk to look at him closely. "Are you sure you are okay?"

Jayce dragged his eyes from her lips and looked into her eyes. *No, I am not okay. What kind of witchcraft are you practicing on me? I can't get you out of my head!*

"Yes, I am sure," he said too loudly. "I am fine."

"The landscaper..." Abigail prompted. "What should I tell the landscaper?"

"Tell him I don't care," Jayce said. "I want to fill the pool, add some trees and flowers. Tell him to run amok. I don't really know about these things; that's why I hired a landscaper. Wait, I definitely want an orange tree. I love oranges."

"But..."Abigail bit her lip, "it's such a nice place, almost half an acre. Don't you want to choose your trees and colorful shrubs and place your bougainvilleas at the side of the fence so that you'll have a burst of color when you enter the driveway?"

Jayce shrugged. "Couldn't care less." A light came in his eyes. "But since you feel so passionate about it, you can talk to him. That's more than fine with me. I'd give you a lift to the house and you could have a ball."

"You would leave it up to me?" Abigail raised her eyebrows and looked at him skeptically.

"Yes, why not?" Jayce said. "My landscape could do with a female touch." *My life could do with a female touch,* he thought silently. *Not just any female, yours.*

Abigail straightened up. "I'll come over to your place this evening and help you make some decisions regarding your landscape then."

Jayce couldn't believe what he was hearing. She was actually offering to help him, after making him depressed over the past two weeks because of her cold treatment. She even had a smile on her face now and was looking at him kindly.

"Okay," he agreed hurriedly. "That'd be great."

*****

Abigail went back to her desk, her heart doing a little tripping dance. She had valiantly tried to resist Jayce for two whole weeks. It hadn't been easy to do; he was equal parts charming and friendly, and it had taken all of her self-control to thwart his advances. It hurt her to be so cold to him but she couldn't risk letting him in on her secret. Jayce was too honest and down to earth to be caught up in the intrigue that was her past life.

She wished she could confide in him, though. Sometimes like now, when she could see his obvious attraction to her, she wished she could pour out her heart to him and have him reassure her that everything was going to be all right.

In the meantime, the least she could do was to be as efficient as possible and help him with his work here. If she could make his personal life any easier without imposing too much, she would be willing to do just that. She had to keep the boundaries between her and Jayce high because he obviously liked her. He had said as much.

She sat at her desk and worried her lips between her teeth, only snapping to attention when the phone rang.

*****

"I had no idea that you knew so much about shrubs and trees and where to put them. You had the landscaper salivating at your suggestions," Jayce said to Abigail.

After they had seen the landscaper, they were sitting at the back of the house on the steps of the empty pool area. It was late evening and the air was cool and the community silent.

Abby shrugged. "There was a time when I dealt with that kind of thing a lot."

Jayce looked at her keenly. She had taken off her sensible work shoes. Her toenails were painted a delicate shade of pink and her pencil skirt was hiked up on her legs. She was sitting beside him, calmly swinging her legs and giving him some insight into her life. He didn't want to ruin it but he wanted to know more. His curiosity about her was at an all-time high. Her terse resume had been no help and she didn't give references—she had a big secret.

"Where?" he asked simply, not making eye contact and trying to be as casual as he could. He was treating her as calmly as one would treat a wild animal, not wanting it to retreat.

"I was married to an extremely wealthy man who had property all over the globe. I was the one who coordinated the landscape. I love that kind of thing. He allowed me to do what I wanted with the places..."

Jayce slowly turned his head toward her. "You were married?"

Abby sighed. "Yes."

"To an extremely wealthy man?"

Abby stopped swinging her legs and looked uncomfortable. "Yes."

"So..." Jayce shook his head in disbelief, "why were you a waitress at Searock? And why are you working for me now?"

Abby grimaced. "It's a long story."

"Obviously," Jayce said, "but we have time. Who is he?" His interest piqued almost to the bursting point. "Why did you two break up?"

Abby cupped her hand in her chin. "I don't want to talk about it. Most of that part of my life I can't tell you about."

"What can you tell me?" Jayce asked.

"I like you," she said earnestly, giving him one of her heart-melting smiles. "I really do, and I am grateful for the job."

Jayce looked at her in disbelief. "You realize that this is classic deflection. You don't want to answer so you give me a compliment and hope that my ego will take over. I am wasting my time with you, aren't I?"

Abby sighed. "I wouldn't say you are wasting your time, I just can't imagine why you find me so interesting, and I can't believe you haven't had a girlfriend since high school. Why did you break up with her?"

"So we are going to talk about me instead," Jayce asked, "when you just dropped a bombshell about your past?"

Abby shrugged. "Or we don't have to talk at all."

Jayce gazed at the stubborn expression on her face and then shrugged. "I'll play along for now, but in the near future I am going to want to know and you are going to tell me."

Abby groaned. "Okay then... Tell me about your great love

for this girl from high school?" She emphasized the word love mockingly.

"Don't mock me," Jayce warned. "I really did love her. Young love can be powerful. I met her when I was sixteen. We were together for four years, we were almost inseparable, and then she left home as soon as she was eighteen.

"I was overseas at college at the time and she never said goodbye to me. I understood why she wouldn't tell anybody else, especially her parents, but to just leave without saying a word to me...the lack of closure haunted me for years. I felt like I couldn't move on without knowing what I did wrong. I mean, we were perfect together—at least that's what I thought."

He shrugged. "She was actually the second woman who I cared about who left me without a proper goodbye."

Abby blinked her eyes rapidly, as if she was fighting back tears. "Who was the first?" she asked huskily.

"My mother," Jayce said. "She left me and my dad. She didn't even pack her clothes or much of her belongings. So for years my dad and I left everything exactly how she had it, hoping that she would come back."

"That's terrible," Abigail said earnestly. "Did you ever find out where she went?"

Jayce nodded. "Yes, a couple of years ago when my dad swallowed his pride and decided to check her out, he found out that she is alive and well, living in the UK. She has another family. Apparently she left us because she had met someone else."

The evening sun was slowly sinking into the horizon. They could hear the melodious chorus of crickets as they heralded the dusk.

Jayce turned to Abigail fully. "My dad has never remarried, nor does he date. He used to jokingly say that the Morgan men are like pigeons."

"How so?" Abigail asked.

"They mate for life and if one dies the survivor accepts a new mate only slowly. I thought Haley was my life-mate but obviously I was wrong and maybe high school was too soon a time to know when you've found the right person. I don't know."

Abigail gasped and then tried to cover it up with a cough.

"What?" Jayce asked. "You find me ridiculous don't you?"

"No." Abby shook her head vigorously. "It's just that...I don't think I am worthy to fit into the shoes of your Haley. I can't be a perfect girlfriend. I have too much baggage for that. I don't even think I want a relationship."

She looked at him apprehensively. "Why do you even like me?"

"Honestly, I have no idea," Jayce said, frowning. "You are pretty, yes, but so are a dozen other girls out there. I don't know if I can explain it but when I saw you in the restaurant, it was your first day there. I remember thinking how I hadn't seen you before. You smiled at me, remember, as if you were waiting for me.

"At the time the only thought in my head was how much seeing you made something in me click. I was irresistibly drawn to you. I have only ever felt this way about Haley. I actually sat down in that restaurant chair, thankful that nothing was wrong with me. It's just like my father said; I must have a pigeon's heart or something."

Abigail jumped up hurriedly, a haunted cast to her face. "Can you take me home now?"

Jayce got up much slower. "Sure." His voice had a defeated tone. He could feel her slipping away from him. She probably thought that he was too intense, too crazy. He may have come on too strong, and why did he have to tell her about Haley? Obviously, his pigeon talk had scared her. It was too much too soon.

He was busily castigating himself when they walked toward the house and the automatic lights came on. Abigail stumbled over a piece of debris and he spun around just in time to help her up.

"Thanks," she said sheepishly. She looked into his eyes. With his back to the lights she couldn't really see his expression, but she could feel the hammering of his heart so close to where her hands rested.

Jayce didn't want to let her go. He inhaled her scent. She smelled faintly like vanilla, or was it citrus? He drew her unresisting body even closer to him and lowered his lips to hers; they were slightly opened and he kissed the gasp that she made.

Their surroundings disappeared, and the world outside no longer existed. For Jayce her arms felt like home, so different and yet so familiar. He trembled with anticipation as she pressed herself closer to him and wound her hand around his neck.

"Haley," he whispered roughly, dragging his lips from hers after what seemed like an interminable time and setting her back from him. He stumbled to the wall and leaned on it, using it as a prop because he had no strength left in his legs.

He looked at Abigail with confusion in his eyes; in his arms. She felt so much like Haley. It had been impossible for his senses to separate the two of them.

Abigail had a stunned look on her face as she stared at him. After a long time she cleared her throat but her voice wasn't quite steady. "Can you take me home now, please?"

Jayce took in a long deep breath. "I am sorry for calling you Haley."

"No worries," Abigail said flippantly. Her voice was still

quivery. "I underestimated your high school love." She walked to his car rapidly and stood at the passenger door, waiting for him impatiently.

He opened her door and ensured that she got into the vehicle, glancing at her closed expression before he walked around to his side.

Jayce felt like an A-class idiot and was horrified at what he had done. He hadn't kissed a girl in such a long time that he couldn't remember what it was like, but the first thing he did was call her by another girl's name.

They were silent all the way to her home. He blamed his dad for convincing him that he had a pigeon's heart. He blamed himself for being so closed off to women that he had only now found someone that he wanted to be with. He blamed Haley and her longevity. She had taken up so much space in his memory that after so long he couldn't even kiss another woman without remembering her.

By the time they pulled up at Golden Gate Apartments Abigail had already taken off her seatbelt and had her hand on the door handle.

"I really am sorry," Jayce said softly.

"Don't sweat it," Abigail said hurriedly as she exited the vehicle. "See you at work tomorrow. We should forget all of this and pretend that it didn't happen."

"No, no, no," Jayce moaned under his breath as she walked away. She fumbled in her bag for her keys, missing the lock several times before she actually got the key in.

She went inside, giving him one last unfathomable look, and then closed her door.

He heaved a sigh; at least she hadn't slammed it. He stayed locked in position, looking at the closed door for the longest while before he drove away.

Chapter Seven

Abby had her ear to the door and when she finally heard the car start up, she breathed a ragged sigh of relief and slumped on the door. How was it possible for Jayce to recognize her after all these years?

She had extensive plastic surgery done on her face. She was sure that even her own mother would pass her in the streets and not recognize her, but Jayce had on some subliminal level known it was her.

That kiss had triggered something in his subconscious because he had called her Haley. It was like an invisible thread drew them together.

Jayce was right; he was like a pigeon and without even realizing it, he had laid bare her deepest secret, without batting an eyelid, and she had made him feel bad about it. She had to.

She staggered to a mirror, looking at her face keenly. Her lips were slightly swollen. That kiss had gone on forever;

she had felt like holding onto Jayce and never letting go. It must have brought back memories of their past. Their lips had met in a familiar passionate dance. It was as if they were back in the nineties again. The kiss had been new and yet familiar.

She touched her lips, backed away from the bathroom, and sat on her bed. She had tried hard not to give Jayce any clues about herself. How was she to know that he remembered her favorite color, the fact that she ate porridge with raisins and inane things like that? The guy had an elephant brain and he had only had her in his life as a girlfriend.

She got up and took off her clothes slowly. She had to tread carefully with him from now on. He was too smart for her and her little clues about her life, which she thought would head him off, but they only made him more curious.

She lay on the bed and closed her eyes. That picture she saw on Jayce's kitchen wall the other night was one she had taken after the band's first fund raising concert.

She had just gotten the camera. It was a professional model she had gotten from her uncle, who had been selling out his belongings to go on a mission trip to Africa. He had given it to her and told her to build memories with it.

Her first picture had been that one of the guys in the band. She had taken another picture that evening; she wondered who had it. She had asked a passerby to take a picture of the guys in the band with their girlfriends.

She had stood beside Jayce, hugging him possessively. Alice had done the same to Carson and Aaron had reluctantly hugged Keisha, who he was slightly afraid of. That year Keisha had been extremely possessive and Aaron had asked her and Alice to break up with Keisha for him that night.

She chuckled silently. Oh, she missed them. When she was forced to leave, the very thought of the band and especially

Jayce had brought her to tears. They had become more than friends; they were family. They had made her life semi-bearable with her overbearing, strict, out-of-touch father.

To stop herself from hurting she had tried to block out that part of her life. For years she forced herself to forget. What good would it do to rehash her days with them? She had naively thought she wouldn't see them again.

She had naively thought that she wouldn't see Jayce again neither. However, when it came time for her survival, she had subconsciously made a decision to return to the one place she knew that she would find him again.

She opened her eyes, staring at the shadows on the wall. Was that why she had returned to Montego Bay? Hadn't she been happy when she found out that he had not moved on? Didn't her heart soar every time he told her how much he couldn't get over Haley? Didn't she feel a secret frisson of pleasure every time she saw what an impact she had had on him?

Yes, yes, yes and yes. She answered her own questions and closed her eyes, permitting herself to remember. She had fought it valiantly for two weeks but tonight, at least tonight, she could indulge her memories a little.

June 1996

"Why on earth is your father so strict?" Jayce asked in exasperation. "You are sixteen years old, not two!" They were lying in separate hammocks in his backyard. "All I did was ask him if you could spend the day with me. He acted as if I asked him permission for you to spend the night. If my father hadn't shown up at church to get me that evening in his fierce military uniform and looked like a hulking menace and assured him that he would be here chaperoning the two of us, he wouldn't have agreed."

Haley giggled. "I give you two thumbs up for bravery for even asking him."

"He must know by now that you and I are friends. You know what, he should know that you are my girlfriend!" Jayce sat up in the hammock; it swung wildly at his sudden movement. "I am going to tell him."

"No." Haley looked alarmed. "My dad is sensitive about boys and stuff. You know that."

"But for God's sake, why?" Jayce asked.

"Because," Haley stressed, "my older sisters both got pregnant before the end of high school."

"Both of them?" Jayce asked.

"Yes," Haley sighed. "Beatrice got pregnant pretty young; her boyfriend was a pastor's kid too. Both parents came together and arranged the marriage so fast your head would spin. That was eight years ago. I had to listen in at doors to hear what was going on. No one would tell me why Beatrice was crying around the place like her world was ending."

Jayce laughed. "Really?"

"Yep." Haley picked up her water bottle and had a sip. "Beatrice and Leon are unhappy together but both parental units would have a fit if the word divorce was even mentioned.

"My other sister, Cher, named for the singer because I think my mother loved her work secretly, did the worst thing."

"What?" Jayce asked, getting into the story.

"Last year she went to camp and sneaked out without telling anyone. So happens that she came home pregnant. She hid it from our parents until after graduation and she wouldn't say who the boy or man was who knocked her up, so my parents pretended that my mother was pregnant. That's why they moved to Montego Bay and my dad gave up his congregation in Kingston. The plan was when the baby was born my mom could pretend that it was hers."

"Are you serious?" Jayce asked, wide-eyed. "Where is Cher now?"

"She took her baby and ran," Haley said. "She was having none of the lie and apparently the guy wanted his child. So you can guess that since I am the youngest and last girl, I am being watched like a hawk.

"My father is terrible at home. I grew up hearing that boys are scum. My mother stands by and does nothing while I am being disciplined for the least little thing, especially if I so much as mention a boy's name. I tell you, if I were different I'd rebel to teach them a lesson."

Jayce subsided back in the hammock and held out his hands to her. They held hands tightly.

"I want to marry you, Haley, and I am not scum," Jayce said solemnly after a long silence.

"When would we get married?" Haley giggled. "Let's see, I am sixteen now. You are eighteen. I go to college in two years. I don't know about marriage now."

"I meant in the future," Jayce looked at her with adoration in his eyes. "I think you are the only girl for me."

Haley smiled. "I think you are the only guy for me too."

She got up from her hammock and lay on top of Jayce, her long skirt wrapping around his legs. Her father made sure that she dressed like a frump most of the time and today was no exception.

She was in a long, shapeless skirt that was impossibly hot in the summer time. She was thinking of keeping a separate wardrobe at Jayce's house, with modern clothes that girls her age wore. She was saving up her lunch money to buy different pieces.

"I'll wear a forest green wedding dress," Haley said softly, resting her head on his rapidly beating heart.

"And we'll march to *Ain't it Enough* by Maxi Priest," Jayce said, kissing her on her forehead.

Haley wrinkled her nose. "My dad would veto that. *Oh Perfect Love* is more his style."

"He'd veto your forest green wedding dress." Jayce retorted. "He would insist on white since you are his only daughter to legitimately wear white at a wedding, and he would want to see your virgin's blood on the sheets before he rested that night."

They both chuckled.

Haley looked up at Jayce. "Your eyes are so sexy."

"Sexy?" Jayce mused. "That is a bad, bad word, Miss Greenwald, it contains sex."

"I mean it." Haley crawled up his chest until she was nose to nose with him. She stared at his lips.

"Are you trying to end up like your sisters?" Jayce whispered. "Pastor Greenwald would definitely kill me."

"No," Haley smiled, "I just want to kiss you."

"Kiss?" Jayce said, alarmed. "You do understand that my dad is in the house, don't you?"

"Yep, but he is watching TV," Haley giggled. "I want you to kiss me like in the movies. Teach me."

Jayce cleared his throat. "You do realize that I have no experience whatsoever about how that goes, don't you?"

"Let's learn together." Haley pressed her lips to his.

They tasted like the soda pop that she had been drinking earlier. He opened his mouth to hers and they quickly learned what it felt like to kiss. They were so lost in their exploration of each other that it was only when The General cleared his throat above them that they broke apart.

"Break it up," The General said sternly.

They both looked at him guiltily. "You two, in the house

in two minutes, when you get yourselves together," he said gruffly.

Haley smoothed back her hair and got up from the hammock. "Is he going to beat us?" She had a look of fear in her eyes.

"No!" Jayce said, getting up from the hammock. "My father wouldn't do that. I can't remember ever getting a beating from him when I was younger, much less now that I am eighteen. Relax."

He linked his arms to hers.

"Is he going to tell my dad?"

"I doubt it," Jayce said worriedly. His father had unconventional ways of making a point: demonstrations and reenactments. His father was a closet drama king. Jayce hoped he didn't scare Haley with his no-holds-barred way of doing things.

When they entered the living room where The General was sitting, he said to them, "Sit down." He indicated the chair before him.

He was drinking a very tall bottle of water and he took several big gulps before he pointed at the two of them. Beads of sweat were gathering on his forehead. He and Jayce shared the same hooded eyes and straight nose; his thick, level brows looked like they were groomed. Haley was looking at him fearfully and expecting him to explode at any minute.

"You two have to get the talk."

"Oh no, Dad," Jayce said, shuddering. "You gave me the talk already."

"But the only thing left for you two to do out there was to remove your clothes and then fit all the parts together," The General said sternly, "in the backyard, in broad daylight with Miss Green's poodle looking on. Anyway, this talk is mostly for Haley." His father drank from the bottle again and after a short pause said, "I have a very strong suspicion that your father has a stick up his anus where sex is concerned."

Haley nodded and giggled.

"Here are the facts." The General put down the water. "Sex is a bonding agent like glue. I guess God made it so to develop a special intimacy with that special someone. It's also a lovely experience; don't listen to the prudes and the naysayers who talk about it like it's something dirty. I guess they never got good loving."

Haley choked with laughter.

Jayce just rolled his eyes. He was used to his father's frank, no-holds-barred, blunt way of speaking.

"Sex is sweet, or it can be sweet with the right person and done in the right setting and I believe at the right age." The General cleared his throat. "It's also an incredible responsibility because it comes with reproductive ties and it is also one of the easiest ways to get diseases. Serious diseases. I don't believe in the new age way of just giving young people condoms and telling them to be careful.

"I think adults should tell them what an awesome responsibility it is to be bonded with another person before they dispense protection. Adults love the easy way out too much because they hate dealing with the sex topic and maybe because they messed up in their own sexual relationships.

"So Haley," he looked at her kindly, "I trust Jayce. He's my boy but I know he has serious feelings for you and I know you have feelings for him and sometimes you both may want to go further than kissing.

"All I am saying is that you both consider the consequences. You are both too young to even know if you'll end up together and so I beseech you not to go further than kissing until you both know for sure what you are getting yourself into.

"You may go now," he said, fanning them away. He picked

up the remote.

Jayce looked at Haley. She had an embarrassed grin on her face.

"That's it?" she whispered when they were in the backyard, once more swinging in the hammock.

"No," Jayce said wryly. "That was it for you. For the rest of the week I am going to get spontaneous lectures about sex and sexually transmitted diseases, and he is going to show me pictures of diseased vaginas at breakfast." He groaned. "I am too old for diseased vaginas at breakfast. It is going to be super weird."

"I wish I had your dad," Haley said feelingly. "My dad is abusive and he gets all weird when he hears the word sex. Even diseased vaginas would be welcome at breakfast instead of what I have to go through now."

"My father is as straight-shooting as they come. He is pretty okay, isn't he?" Jayce grudgingly admitted.

"Yep." Haley got up from her hammock and came to lie on top of him again. "It's better over here."

"Isn't it?" Jayce murmured, holding her closer to him.

*****

Abigail was jerked from her memories when a car door slammed outside her door. She hugged her other pillow close to her and closed her eyes, imagining that the pillow was Jayce. She had always loved to cuddle up to him.

She needed to sleep. She could feel the dragging weariness behind her eyes. She wished that she were in a quieter community like where Jayce lived. She wondered if he was sleeping now or if he was thinking about her when she was younger or now when she was older, with a different face.

She wondered who he found more attractive, her or Haley.

She then realized how absolutely ridiculous her thoughts were. She drifted off into a troubled sleep.

Chapter Eight

Jayce got up at dawn, fifteen minutes before his alarm went off. He hadn't slept much last night. He groggily dragged his gym clothes from a basket in the corner of the huge master bedroom. The room only had his two suitcases, his laundry basket, and a double bed, which looked ridiculously small in the master bedroom that could comfortably hold a king-sized bed.

He washed his clothes over at Logan's house these days. Melody had recently sent over his basket with the clothes all folded neatly and color-coordinated. He ruffled through the neat stack, pulling clothes out without regard for the order in which she had placed them. He offered a silent, groggy apology to Melody for the disregard to her much-appreciated work.

He stumbled to the bathroom and brushed his teeth. He needed to do some things today. He needed to see about furnishing his house. He needed to build a backbone where

Abigail was concerned and do as she said and forget that he had kissed her and called her Haley, and he needed to work on un-liking her.

He couldn't be in a cloak and dagger kind of relationship where he had to wade through secrets and games; that was not his type of thing. He wondered if he could accomplish un-liking Abigail.

He looked in the mirror. His eyes still looked sleepy but this morning was The General's morning for them to go jogging on the beach. Losing weight had been the easy part, he realized, while stretching and trying to dislodge the kink that was in his neck. He yawned widely instead and looked at his bed longingly.

What sort of madness had gripped him to want to look as ripped and athletic as his father and his friends? Every one of them looked like they had stepped off the cover of some girlie magazine and he thought that he should too.

He lifted his shirt and looked at his abs front on. He could already see the definition, where hopefully a six-pack would emerge. His belly was wondrously flat now; he hadn't seen it like that since his early twenties. It had a puckered scar where the bullet had grazed him—his war wound. Not even The General had one of those.

He flexed his biceps and found that there was some power behind them. They were not as big as Ian's, but surely they were comparable to Logan's? He moved from the mirror and headed downstairs to the kitchen for a banana. His father hammered on the door before he could reach the kitchen, and he opened it.

"Morning General," he said, blinking rapidly as the cool air from the morning came rushing in. "You look to be in fine form today."

"Morning," his father growled. "You still look sleepy."

"Rough night," Jayce said over his shoulder as he headed for the kitchen. "I couldn't settle. Can we go lighter today? Have some pity on me."

"No." The General looked shocked at his request. "Sleep or no, privates have to be ready for the battlefield and they have to be alert."

"But the thing is," Jayce said, swallowing the banana in two bites, "we are not at war. I am just a regular old civilian with woman problems."

"Really?" his father said. "You have finally found a woman? I was beginning to worry about you."

"Why?" Jayce said, grabbing his water bottle.

"Because, you know," his father shrugged, "you are thirty-four. When a man is single and still a virgin at thirty-four one gets concerned. Especially if you aren't looking for a partner and have no desire to...er...find one. I must admit I saw my lineage stopping with you. "

"I should never have told you last year that I was a virgin," Jayce sighed. "You bring it up in every single conversation. I ask you what you are drinking you say virgin *Daiquiri*, virgin smoothie, virgin water and then give me the side-eye like I am a freak. You are partly responsible for me still being a virgin, with your constant emphasis on sex being meaningful and me having a pigeon heart and all of that nonsense."

"I was teasing," his father chuckled, "and I still stand by what I said. I applaud you for it, even. In this day and age you are a pearl among men."

"Pearl among men. Really?" Jayce shook his head. "I don't trust you when you get poetic."

"So who's the woman?" his father asked when they stepped outside and Jayce locked the front of the house.

"Abigail," Jayce said sheepishly. "I kissed her last night and called her Haley. I was an idiot."

His father chuckled. "Abigail, your secretary? She's a beauty, isn't she?"

"Yes," Jayce said, "and you are missing the point. I called her Haley."

"Then tell her that Haley is an old, old, old high school friend and your subconscious made a mistake." The General frowned. "Surely she'll understand."

The General picked up pace as they walked downhill toward the beach. At this time in the morning, only a few vehicles were on the road. They passed other die-hard joggers who were struggling up the hill.

Jayce said worriedly, "I think I am making all the wrong moves with Abby and I think she is withdrawing from me. Added to that, she's so mysterious. I don't know anything about her background, family, friends—nothing. The only thing I know is that she was once married to a wealthy man, she eats raisins with her porridge and she loves landscaping."

The General looked at him, puzzled. "You didn't do a background check on her like you said you would, did you?"

"No," Jayce said, "I wanted her to confide in me. I didn't want to go snooping in her life like some kind of peeping tom."

"She works for us, Jayce." They crossed the road together and walked on rocks down to the sand. "You know we have a strict policy about researching backgrounds. How did I make that slip?"

"Because I told you I'd do it," Jayce said sullenly.

"Do it!" his father said, heading off down the beach. "Maybe then she'll not be so mysterious to you."

Jayce ran effortlessly to keep pace with his father, something that he thought he wouldn't be able to do in a million years.

*****

Jayce entered the office earlier than usual. Abigail wasn't in yet, nor did he expect her to be. He was the only one in the building apart from the security guards in the lobby. He had taken up most of the six-mile run with his father thinking about Abigail Petri.

He had promised her that he wouldn't have his father snoop into her background but he hadn't said he wouldn't. He was approaching this on a technicality but he felt guilty about doing it.

He sat at his computer and brought up her information from HR. Abigail Petri, Age 28, Birthday: Feb 1, Previous Employers: Searock Cafe, 1 year. No references. The Golden Gate address. Her resume was as uninformative and as dry as he had thought the moment he had seen it. There was nothing new on it, nothing that he didn't already know.

He logged into the Intelligence Network and entered her name. If she had worked for anyone else, had a credit card, email address, used the Internet or anything like that, he would have access to that information.

After he hit enter a pang of regret found its way to the surface of his mind. It should not have come to this; he shouldn't have to search like this and ferret out information about her like she was some criminal. He saw two Abigail Petris come up on the screen. The first one had a Kingston address. That was it. She had no credit history, no work history—nothing.

The second one was 86 years old and had a nursing home address. He frowned at the screen. Nobody lived off the grid in this day and age, unless they had something to hide or were so old fashioned that they left no trace in a database somewhere. This was what his father would call a red flag.

In the normal course of doing a background check, Abigail Petri would have been a code red. Highly likely to be a person involved in fraud.

He closed his eyes and swung in his chair gently. What had he gotten himself into?

What was she hiding, and more importantly, who was she?

"Hey Jayce." He cracked his eye open. It was Rashida, their newest staff member. She was a corporate security investigator. She was waving to him from the door.

"Hey Rashida," he smiled at her pleasantly. "You are here ridiculously early."

Today was her first official day. She had gotten the tour from HR yesterday and had seemed quite pleasant. He looked at her. She was fresh out of university and still had that eager-eyed spark about her that indicated that she was ready for anything.

Rashida walked farther into his office. She looked sleek and sophisticated with her shoulder length, thick hair cupping her face lovingly and her finely-tailored pantsuit hinting at a sleek shape. She was gorgeous and she knew it.

He felt himself tense up imperceptibly when she gazed at him a look of attraction blazing from her eyes. He had seen it yesterday and had studiously avoided it. He hoped she wasn't going to be a problem. He had been propositioned quite a few times by various women on the staff, even when he was fat and thought himself unattractive. He knew that there was a special allure about him simply because he was the owner's son.

Rashida sat across from his desk and grinned. "Your chairs are super comfy."

"Thanks," Jayce said. "How is it going?"

"I just got in and decided to have a look around by myself. You guys have fifteen different tea flavors in the cafeteria kitchen," she gushed. "That's amazing. I didn't even know that people could drink orange peels. There's a tea bag marked orange peels."

"You didn't know that?" Jayce said laughingly. "How come? The whole world knows. Orange peels have a host of nutrients in them. At least that's what my father used to tell me when he forced me to drink what I call his vile brews."

Rashida laughed. "Your dad is awesome. I really like him."

"You do?" Jayce raised his eyebrows.

"I can't believe he is your father. He looks so young."

Jayce was on the verge of snickering. He looked at Rashida as she bit her plump red lips. He hoped she wasn't angling to be his stepmother. It would be funny to see The General fight off Rashida's attention.

"Is this the time you come in?" Rashida asked him, crossing her legs daintily. "I would think that as the boss' son you would have special privileges."

Jayce laughed. "I do have special privileges, but I have to work twice as hard as a stranger because ultimately I want the business to succeed. That's all the special privilege I have."

"What are you doing this weekend?" Rashida asked, changing the subject, "I have two tickets to the Natural Life Festival."

She was asking him out? Her first day here and she was already making a play for him and wasn't even batting an eyelid about it.

If only Abigail were like this: open, man hungry, and bold, he would welcome her warmly.

"Sorry," Jayce said regretfully. "I am already going. My band is performing there."

"Oh. Yes. You sing in the New Song band." Rashida mused, "I'll just have to find someone else to go with, then.

It sounds like it is going to be great. I think more people, including myself, need to live healthier lives. I can't wait to see what they have on display there. I heard that they are also going to show off an eco friendly house."

Jayce said half jokingly, "Why don't you ask my dad to go?"

"You think he would go with me?" Rashida asked breathlessly.

"Yes. Why not?" Jayce said. "He loves that kind of thing. Why do you think he looks so young? He is a vegan-loving, orange peel-drinking kind of guy. And he totally digs solar energy and what not."

"Okay," Rashida inhaled. "I will ask him. Wish me luck."

Jayce nodded, a mischievous twinkle in his eyes. "I say go with God and tread carefully, The General can be… er, abrasive."

He watched as Rashida jumped up with a determined look in her eyes. He wondered when she was going to make a play for his father because he would not mind sticking around to see it.

*****

"Jayce," Abigail said tentatively. He looked up, trying to affect an air of disinterest. He heard when she got in at eight. Usually she would push her head around the door and greet him, but she hadn't done so this morning, so he knew she must have been psyching up herself to see him after their tremendously awkward time yesterday.

"Yes." He looked up at her from the line of computer code he was typing; he was fine-tuning the prototype that Xavier had sent to him.

"You have a whole slew of messages. I was wondering..."

"Just handle the things that can be handled by you," he said tersely. "Leave the rest in my tray." He pointed to it.

He had been practicing his tone all morning before she got in for work; he had dubbed it the efficient business approach. Of course, he had also seen that she was wearing green today, forest green.

What irony. It was Haley's favorite color; he had called her Haley after that earth-shattering kiss last night. He also noticed that her eyelashes were thick and stubby; she had on mascara, which made them look even wider.

He looked back down at his computer. He didn't want to catalogue her features; next he'd be noticing her lips and the way her eyebrows slanted at just the right angle or her pale pink nails and how they clutched the note pad.

"Are you free this evening? A Mr. Junip would like a..."

"Band practice is at five on Wednesdays," Jayce growled. "Never schedule anything or anyone for that time."

He felt bad when she flinched at his tone but he was mad at himself and his reaction to her. What was it about her that he found so irresistible? She was just a woman. He had seen thousands of women in his lifetime but she had to be the one he found fascinating.

"About last night..." Abby said reluctantly.

"I thought we were never going to mention that again," Jayce said, looking at her coldly. "I am sorry I called you Haley. I am sorry I shared my feelings with you. I'll try not to let it happen again."

"Are you mad at me for something?" Abby asked.

"No," Jayce shook his head, "mad at myself."

Abby sighed. "I can help you pick out furniture for your house if you like. I see you have it on your list of things to do." She pointed to a post-it note that he had on his desk.

Jayce stiffened. "I don't think it's a good idea. I like you,

Abby. If you pick out furniture and help me decorate my place, when you go out of my life I'll have the memories. I'll pick up a towel and remember that you chose it. I don't want to go through that again."

"I don't have any plans to go anywhere," Abby said stubbornly.

"Is that so?" Jayce said exasperatedly. "Well, you can't have it both ways. You can't keep me at arms' length and then kiss me passionately whenever the mood suits you."

"You kissed me," Abby pointed out.

"And you kissed me back, thoroughly," Jayce said, his eyes straying to her lips; memories of how they felt dangled across his mind.

"And I reminded you of Haley," Abigail said accusingly.

His phone rang and he breathed a sigh of relief. He had no idea how he was going to live down the absolute gaffe that he had made last night. It was Aaron on the line; he sounded excited.

"Hi Uncle Jayce, your nephew is here."

"He is!" Jayce laughed, "Congrats, man. I didn't know Alka was in the hospital."

"I rushed her here in the wee hours of the morning," Aaron said, a sound of relief in his voice, "and the little fellow didn't take too long to get here, either. They are at the Lee Wing at the private hospital," he continued. "You know, I have you to thank for them being here with me now."

Jayce groaned. "Aaron, come on. No thanks necessary."

Aaron chuckled. "I am still thanking you. Come down here before band practice. Maybe by then the whole Lee clan will have left. Nonna arranged for everyone to be here with her meddling self.

"By the way, Alka and I decided to call him Christian. It was Farrah's idea; she has appointed herself the official 'namer' of the New Song band babies."

He hung up and Jayce put down his phone with a grin on his face. Abigail was staring at him, her eyebrows raised.

"My friend Aaron is a dad," Jayce explained. "Aaron sings with me in the New Song band."

"And you guys are like brothers." Abigail nodded. "So you are an uncle now?"

Jayce nodded. "Yes, once more. He has a son."

Abigail smiled, her eyes lighting up in genuine happiness. "I am happy for him and his wife, of course."

Jayce pointed at her. "That was a warm smile for a guy you do not even know. Why can't you smile at me that way?"

Abby schooled her face into seriousness lines and fidgeted with her note pad. "I like to hear when people are happy."

"Really?" Jayce frowned. "Well then, if you go with me to the Natural Life Festival, I'll be over the moon happy. I'll be bristling with so much joy I don't know how I will be able to keep myself grounded to earth."

Abby chuckled. "Okay, I'll go with you. I was planning to go anyway."

"Grudgingly stated but I'll accept anyway," Jayce said. "I am going to knock off early this evening, okay?"

Abigail nodded and then headed to her desk. She sat in her chair, a feeling of loneliness washing over her. She stared at her computer blankly. Aaron's happy news had a dual effect on her. She was genuinely happy for Aaron but at the same time she felt like a ghost, watching the lives of her past friends but not being able to participate.

If life had not taken the turn it had for her, she would most likely be a part of the happy news now. She would probably have bought Aaron's child a gift long before now. She would have visited the hospital with Jayce and cooed over the baby.

She would visit the band practice with him or maybe

hang out with Alice if she was around. Alice was not overly friendly when they were in high school but they had gotten along even then.

She didn't know Ian's wife, Ruby, or Xavier's wife, Farrah, but she was sure that they would be nice friends to have and obviously Logan's wife, Melody, who was the band manager, would be her friend because she cared for Jayce.

Melody called her to check up on Jayce, confessing to Abigail that she was not sure that he was taking care of himself as he should. Jayce's near-death experience seemed to have genuinely affected Melody, much more than he knew or could appreciate. She had a feeling all his friends were affected, but Jayce didn't quite realize just how shaken up they had been.

She gave a heartfelt, tremulous sigh and went back to her work, feeling as if she were a nobody. No family, no friends—she just existed behind a strange face.

Chapter Nine

The Natural Life Festival was in full swing when Jayce arrived that Sunday evening. The band was going to play in a concert but he had thought it would be nice to experience a little of what the festival was all about before he joined his friends near the stage area.

Abigail stood beside him. He had picked her up from her home, and they had a pleasant ride over to the park, which was transformed into a veritable organic festival. There was a sea of stalls in the large park, each of them dedicated to some aspect of eating organically or living in an eco-friendly manner.

"I always check out the food first," Abigail said, looking around.

Jayce grinned. "Me too. I may be slimmer but I am a foodie at heart. I want to check out the tech area as well. I hear they are doing some amazing things with solar technology these days."

"There's your dad with Rashida from the office." Abigail pointed in the direction of a gaily-decorated stall with pumpkins.

"I can't believe it." Jayce shook his head. "He actually came with her."

"Let's go check out the pumpkins…" Abigail grinned.

"The General doesn't look happy," Jayce said, chuckling. "Maybe Rashida is too chatty for him."

"Or too young for him?" Abigail said, frowning.

"Hey," Jayce looked at her and raised his eyebrows. "You don't like my dad too? Is that why you don't want to date me?"

Abigail giggled and then she found that when she started she couldn't stop. She had not laughed so hard and with such genuine, unfettered mirth in years—more years than she could remember.

"Jayce," she choked, "you are hilarious. The General is not my type."

Jayce grinned at her. He loved to see her this happy. The thought that her laughter reminded him of Haley was firmly pushed to the back of his mind. He had to let Haley rest some time. This couldn't go on. He could jeopardize everything with Abigail because of his Haley remembrances.

As soon as The General spotted them, he walked over, giving them a hasty greeting. Rashida walked with him, a grin on her face.

The General pulled Jayce to the side and fiercely whispered, "She asked me if I wanted a ticket to the festival. I said yes. I had no idea she would come with me. Take her off my hands, Jayce, or I am firing her tomorrow. Don't think I don't know that you put her up to this. She told me that you said I like orange peel tea."

Jayce saw the fierce determination in his father's eyes and

chuckled. "Relax. Enjoy yourself. Loosen up a little."

The General growled and then turned around to the ladies with a polite smile on his face. "Okay, I am going to the tech area."

He swung around and glowered at Jayce, and they both watched as he strode away quickly, with Rashida half-running to catch up with him.

Abigail started laughing again and Jayce watched her with a smile on his face.

"Before we go to get something to eat, come meet my friends," Jayce said impulsively. "You already met Xavier. I want you to meet the rest of them."

Abigail sobered up quickly. "I'll see them play later. Aren't you guys playing?"

"Yes," Jayce said, a note of exasperation creeping into his voice. "I meant meet them personally."

Abigail shook her head. "Nope, this is like meeting the family. It's like a test. Everyone will check me out and then you will all discuss my merits as soon as I turn my back. Carson will say, 'She looks nice. Is she a Christian?' Ian will say, 'I don't care how she looks. Is she an honest person?'

"Aaron is so grateful and thankful for his new wife and new baby that he will say that once you are happy he is happy as well. Logan will give me the silent, probing stare and then ask if I read. Xavier won't be at the stage area. He is too into technology not to be at that booth; besides, he met me at the restaurant."

She realized her mistake as soon as she was finished doing a summary of the band members' various character traits. Jayce was looking at her with his mouth slightly opened and such a puzzled look on his face that Abigail almost called herself an idiot out loud. She had spoken as someone who knew the guys intimately. She could see the frown line between Jayce's eyes and he stood back from her as if he had seen a ghost.

What seemed like minutes ticked by. Jayce pushed his hands into his pockets and looked down at the ground and then looked across at her. "Have we met before?"

"What?" Abigail asked, her heart skipping a couple of beats; she mimicked his pose and pushed her hands in her jeans. "Why do you ask that?"

"Did me meet before I met you at the restaurant?" Jayce asked slowly. "Do you know my friends?"

Abigail swallowed. "Why would you say that?" she asked with an uncomfortable laugh. "Was I that accurate with what I just said?"

"Too accurate," Jayce said. "You know, the first time he saw you Xavier said you looked familiar to him."

"He did?" Abigail asked incredulously. "Where would he have seen me before?"

"I don't know." Jayce shrugged. "How did you know that Logan has a probing stare?"

"That came off pretty clear from the picture on your wall in your kitchen," Abby shrugged. "Remember…when you guys were younger?"

"It did?" Jayce stepped closer to her. "How do you know that Ian has a fixation with loyalty and honesty?"

"I guessed?" Abigail said slowly. "It's not a big deal, Jayce. I just summed up your friends based on my imagination. Now you are giving me the third degree."

Jayce shook his head. "No, you are not getting away with that defense on this one. You are definitely going to meet them. And I am asking each of them if they have met you before."

"You can't make me," Abigail pouted.

"I can lift you up and carry you over my shoulders," Jayce

said, shrugging. "You are what, a hundred and twenty-five pounds? My father has me dead-lifting more than that at the gym. I can mange you."

Abigail rolled her eyes. "Whatever, man. Lead the way to your friends."

When Jayce entered the backstage area all his friends were there except Xavier. He glanced at Abigail.

Was she a witch? How could she so fluently and efficiently name his friends and their various personalities, almost as if she was familiar with them? It bothered him but that didn't prevent him from holding her hand as they trekked all the way to the stage. He hadn't quite trusted that she wouldn't have run off in the crowd, and besides he liked having her hand in his.

It felt right, perfect somehow, like they had held hands this way before and walked together. He shook his fanciful feelings aside and wondered once more if she was a witch, a fortuneteller, or something.

"Hey Jayce." Ian waved to him. He had his feet propped up on a chair, and he was sipping a drink.

Other artists and bands were milling around and he waved to some of the people that he knew before he made it to the corner that his band had claimed as theirs.

He looked at Abigail suspiciously. "How did you know the names of my friends?"

"That's common knowledge, Jayce. You guys are pretty popular, you know." Abigail widened her eyes at him. "You are really acting strange about my little speech earlier."

"So who is he?" Jayce asked, nodding to Ian.

Ian looked between the two of them, a look of query on his face.

"Ian Scott," Abigail said, smiling and holding out her hand to Ian. "How are you? I am Abigail Petri."

Ian shook her hand and grinned. "Abigail? Now where have I heard that name before?"

"Do you know her from anywhere?" Jayce asked suspiciously.

"No." Ian got up. "Nice to meet you, Abigail."

Carson and Aaron both shook her hand as gleefully as Ian had, and Jayce resisted asking them if they knew her. Obviously, they didn't; they didn't act like it. There was no recognition on any of their faces.

Logan came in shortly after they were in the middle of introductions and shook Abigail's hand briefly and then stared at her assessingly, as she had predicted that he would, but not with any kind of recognition. The whole thing felt weird to Jayce. How had she so fluently summed up their personalities without a blink?

He couldn't shake the question from his mind when they excused themselves and went for a stroll around before the show and their set-up.

"See, I told you that they don't know me," Abigail said to him, grinning.

Jayce nodded. "Yes, you were right and maybe I am a tiny bit paranoid, but you were so accurate."

"So what songs are you performing tonight?" Abigail asked.

"We are opening with *Natural Mystic* by Bob Marley," Jayce said "and of course we'll do a couple of other songs."

"Ah, one of my favorites by him," Abigail said. "Love the words, especially the part, 'Things are not the way they used to be... One and all got to face reality now... '" She started humming it. "Can't wait for you guys to play it."

Jayce shook his head in bemusement. "Wait, I didn't even realize those words were in there. I am just playing guitar to it. Maybe if I was singing I would have played closer attention."

Abigail looked at him. "You seem like the kind of guy to listen to the lyrics of a song."

"I am the kind of guy to listen to the lyrics and obsess over them," Jayce said ruefully. "I am a secret poetry writer. I won't even ask how you know that about me."

"Lucky guess, Jayce. Lighten up. I can't read minds."

"So why do you like that line so much?"

Abigail stopped walking and looked at him intently. "I love the whole song...It is simple, really. That line that says, 'things are not the way they used to be, to me' means that I had to wake up and accept that what I had is long gone. Things are different...things have changed... I have changed.

"It says to me that I should stop trying to regain the past; it will never come back. Stop trying to be someone I'm not and accept the new me and new circumstances that I am working with."

"Wow," Jayce raised his eyebrows.

Tears gathered at the corners of Abigail's eyes and she blinked them away. "That line that says 'one and all got to face reality now' says to me that the first step to becoming a new, better me is accepting that things have changed and I have to give up my desire to go back to another time. It's gone and never coming back. I have to wake up and face reality if I ever want to make progress in this life."

"Wow again," Jayce whispered after Abigail was done speaking.

She dashed a hand over her eyes. "I am sorry, I get..."

"No," Jayce said, pulling her closer to him and hugging her. "Honesty. Don't apologize for it. You do know that I am going to be listening to the entire song and dissecting it, don't you?"

Abigail chuckled against his chest weakly. They stood like

that for the longest time, the crowd milling around them.

Chapter Ten

Jayce sat in his chair and tapped his fingers on his chin. He pondered about yesterday's Natural Life fair where Abigail practically told him a little bit about herself without her even realizing it. She had said that she had changed and the past would never come back. That made him so curious and jittery. He hated mysteries.

He now wanted to know everything about her and he wanted it now. Her ridiculously suspenseful life was literally tying his brain up in knots. He had already called his contacts in Kingston to find the address of the Abigail Petri that he had on the screen. It was an apartment building. Abigail had moved out a year and a half ago. He gritted his teeth in frustration.

She had paid her rent in cash. Apparently she had moved to Montego Bay shortly after. He could hear her outside, in the outer office. Her fingers were moving rapidly over the computer keyboard; he had given her a report to complete a few minutes ago. She had her headphones on and was humming to some music or the other.

He wondered how he could get her to spend some more time with him and open up to him. His eyes fell on the post-it note that he had placed on his desk last week; the first item on there was to buy furniture.

He could easily have gotten Ruby or Melody to help him with furniture shopping. Melody loved those kinds of things and had already hinted that she would like to help him, but so had Abigail a few days ago. There was his opportunity.

He pressed the intercom.

"Abigail could you come to my office, please?" He pulled out the furniture book that he had been browsing through and put it on the desk. Except for his already-done kitchen, he had nothing but his bed. He needed everything.

"Yes," Abigail said, walking into his office. Today she was buttoned up like a schoolmarm in a brown tweed suit. It still looked good on her, though.

"I was thinking," he said, "that if your offer is still standing we could shop for furniture for my place."

"Oh," Abby nodded, "I would like that."

"Is that something you used to do for your ex-husband too?" Jayce asked. He watched as her eyes shuttered and she stiffened. *So the topic of the husband is off limits.* It was good to know; he would have to visit it again.

She pursed her lips, looking at him disapprovingly. "I am so sorry I told you."

"I am happy you did." Jayce grinned. "When are we free for the furniture shopping?"

"The rest of the afternoon is free," Abigail said. "I think we have to discuss a concept first, though. Like what overall feel you want for your place, and then move on from there."

Jayce groaned. He had wanted to spend some time with her

but this was not his type of thing. He couldn't bother with the choices and poring over cloth swatches and what-not. He had seen Melody do that for his kitchen, and he had tired just thinking about it. "Tell you what," he said hurriedly. "I can pay you to be my decorator. You can come over and organize my house as you see fit."

"What about what you said earlier about me not doing it?" Abigail asked skeptically. She folded her arms and gave him her best schoolmarm impersonation. "What are you cooking up in your head?"

"Nothing," Jayce said innocently. "I just changed my mind."

"Are you sure you don't want a professional?" Abigail asked.

Jayce shrugged. "Melody was not a pro and she did a great job with the kitchen. All I did was tell her I liked forest green."

"So why don't you have her do the rest of the house?" Abigail asked, a little pinprick of jealousy sticking her. Melody was heavily involved in Jayce's life. He mentioned her every other minute. Melody did his laundry; Melody made him green juice; Melody loved to cook; Melody took care of him when he was sick.

"It's coming down to the busiest part of the year for her," Jayce interrupted her thoughts. "Besides, if I ask her she'll say yes."

"She sounds like one of those goody two-shoes women who can handle anything with their hands tied behind their back. She's perfect, isn't she?" Abigail said.

"She is." Jayce nodded vigorously and then added, "Perfect for Logan. You sound jealous."

"Nope, not jealous." Abigail said, picking up the furniture book and leafing through, avoiding eye contact.

He handed her his credit card with a pleased glint in his eye.

"Are you working with a budget?" Abby asked grumpily, sore at herself for giving so much away. She was jealous of Melody's role in his life.

Jayce laughed. "No, not really, just don't go overboard. I don't want chandeliers in every room."

"Got it," Abigail said gruffly.

*****

Four weeks. It took Abby four weeks to get everything that she wanted for the place. Abigail looked around Jayce's nicely decorated home and smiled. She had gone to the bigger furniture places, and she had gotten a few pieces custom built, like the tree trunk center table, remnants from the logwood tree that she had the landscaper cut down. She had made Jayce's place into her own place. She hoped he never found out that she had been living out her fantasy while decorating his place.

He seemed to like everything she did, so she hoped it was his fantasy too. They both had similar tastes years ago, so she wasn't been worried that he wouldn't like her work. Jayce was gone to Logan's house to get another box of his stuff to put in the living room. He called them his personal effects. He said Logan had them in his basement for safekeeping. He carted his boxes one by one from the bottom of the street to where he lived. He said it was exercise. He had to go get one more box, but the living room was already filled with them.

She lovingly hung up a picture of Jayce that he took with his father a few weeks ago. She had told him that she wanted a picture of them, in black and white, to match the color scheme for the living room. Now that she had done the place, she didn't want to leave.

She chuckled to herself. She was playing with fire. Over the past weeks, whenever she came over with some decorating idea or the other or ordered the movers where to place furniture, Jayce was usually nearby; she had dinner or lunch with him.

He told her stories about himself, some of which she already knew. She listened to his stories and longed to share her stories with him, but she couldn't.

She couldn't share much and she could see that her lack of sharing was driving Jayce crazy. He asked her pointed questions but she would sidestep them. All he wanted to do was get to know her better. She felt sorry for him that he liked her.

She felt sorry for herself that she liked him still. Loved him still, she corrected softly. She hadn't stopped loving him.

She pulled a box in which Jayce had a whole slew of records and CDs. She estimated that he had more than five hundred CDs; no wonder he had insisted that his record shelf had to be huge and his entertainment system had to have surround-sound. Those had been his only stipulations. She prodded through the box and realized that most of the CDs were classics from the 70s and 80s.

She would start packing his record shelf, and she wondered if he would prefer that she do so by artist or by year.

She paused when she reached a CD case with Maxi Priest. Jayce had loved the song *Ain't it Enough* when they were dating back in the day. It was the only song on the CD. She smiled…typical Jayce. He must have played it repeatedly.

She pushed the CD into his multiplayer entertainment set and pressed play. When the song started, she closed her eyes.

*****

It was in January 1997, the last night before Jayce left for school. She was eighteen, Jayce twenty. He had finished a year and a half at MIT in the States. They had been nearly inseparable over the Christmas holidays.

She had gone against her father's express will and sneaked out to meet Jayce, even in the middle of the night. They would meet at her gate and then they would drive to his house.

His house had been freedom…freedom from oppression and her father's stifling authority. Her father had promised her a college education if she kept her legs closed, as he had so crudely put it. She had studiously been doing her pre-college courses while missing Jayce, toward whom she wrote long sappy letters in her diary every day.

Her parents had gone to a church service when she had invited Jayce over.

"Are you sure I should be over here?" Jayce asked, looking around. "Your dad would have a fit if he knew that I was over here.

"I have a present for you." She drew him into the living room and he looked around curiously. He had never been to her house, even though they had known each other for years.

"You know, I was expecting to see balls and chains," Jayce whispered.

Haley laughed. "You can speak loudly; they are not here."

"I know but the place feels as if I should whisper," Jayce said. "I can feel the specter of your dad in every pore of the room."

When they entered her room Jayce looked around. It was painfully neat and had no pictures whatsoever. It didn't look like a teenage girl's room.

"Are you sure you live here?" he asked jokingly.

"Yep," Haley grinned. "Pictures are graven images according to my father and bright colors or anything of the kind is an abomination to him. Why do you think I like forest green so much, and reds and oranges and anything bright and pretty? My dad caused it. If it were up to him I would only wear beige and bland colors."

Jayce hesitantly sat on the bed. "Haley, I am not comfortable being in here."

"I know." Haley winked at him. She went into her closet, which also looked neat. "I got you this."

She inhaled and clutched the CD to her chest. "I asked one of my friends to help me get it done."

She handed the CD to him. It was Maxi Priest's album, *Man With The Fun*, but it had her face on the front of it. She had on makeup. Her hair was out in a defiant afro cloud around her face. She looked so pretty and grown up.

Jayce looked up at her. "I am going to take out the picture and then play the CD. Thank you, Haley."

"You are welcome." She giggled and sat beside him. "There's a letter in the back for you to read when you are at school. The picture is for when you see any pretty girls around campus. You just look at it and remember me."

Jayce drew her closer to him. "I love you so much. I doubt I can forget you. Ever."

"You better mean it." She looked up at him and then whispered, "Kiss me, Jayce."

"Not in the lion's den," Jayce said hoarsely.

He lowered his lips to hers, though, and held her even tighter to him. She pulled him toward her, lying on the bed with Jayce kissing her thoroughly.

"I knew it!" The bellow from the door was like a gunshot. They drew apart so fast Haley felt breathless and dizzy at the same time.

"I would ask you to leave my premises, Jayce Morgan," Greenwald said, gritting his teeth.

Jayce looked at Haley, concerned. He knew that her father was abusive. He knew that he still beat her for the slightest infractions. He was reluctant to leave. She had a scared look on her face, like she was deathly afraid.

"Look Mr. Greenwald," he said weakly, "I don't think..."

"Then don't think," Greenwald said almost pleasantly. "Leave my premises, now!"

Jayce clutched the CD to him; he knew that if Greenwald saw it, it would be further hell for Haley. He wished that he didn't have to leave her. She had recently turned eighteen; she could leave with him.

"Let's leave now, Haley," he urged, genuinely fearful for her.

Haley swallowed. She knew what was going to happen next but she couldn't leave with Jayce. It would be worse if she did.

"No. Go," she said to Jayce weakly.

When Jayce left reluctantly, her father slammed the front door and then he bellowed. "Hannah! Didn't I tell you that this last girl was cut out to be a harlot like all the rest of her sisters? Didn't I tell you? In my own house! I caught her kissing a man. At least her other sisters had enough sense not to carry their men into my house."

Haley listened through the door. It was impossible not to hear him; his preacher's voice was loud and commanding. She also heard his heavy footsteps as they headed for her door.

"You," he said, pointing at her, his eyes wrathful red. "I am going to teach you a lesson you should not forget. If you ever think of contacting that boy Jayce again, I am going to make sure that you remember tonight." He slowly took off his heavy leather belt.

"The Bible says train up a child in the way he should go and when he is older he shall not depart from it. Where have I gone wrong, Lord?" he asked in genuine anguish before he approached her and slapped her across the back with the belt.

"How many times have you kissed that boy, Haley Greenwald? If you lie to me, I will know and I will be avenged."

"I wasn't counting," Haley said weakly.

He nodded, satisfied. "So you have done it so many times you lost count? Have you slept with him?"

"No," Haley said, swallowing. Her throat was constricted and she could feel the sting of the slap against her back.

"Mmmh." He swiped the belt across her back again, putting all his might into it. He was a big man and she was a small girl.

Sometime in the night, after he had finished punishing her for her sins, she had passed out. She had been unable to move in the morning; she had difficulty breathing and she had difficulty unwinding herself from the defensive ball she had contorted herself into to deflect the blows. Her mother's quavering voice had woken her up the morning after the beating.

"Haley." She was shaking her and sobbing. "Thank God you are alive. I thought you were dead. I thought he had killed you. You didn't seem as if you were breathing."

She sniffed, tears streaming down her face. "I am going to send you to your aunt in Kingston. I already called her. You remember your aunt Barbara."

"The forbidden one?" Haley barely whispered.

"Yes." Her mother nodded vigorously. "She is coming to get you. She should be here shortly. I secretly called her last night."

"You can't tell your father where you are. You can't." She sobbed again and then she helped Haley up. "You have to get away from here. He is gone to work."

"Haley," she said as she helped her swollen, almost broken daughter to the bathroom. "Pretend like you are dead. Leave all this behind. Leave this family behind. Leave this town behind. Don't look back. You have to."

"But Jayce..." Haley whispered.

"Jayce doesn't go to school here. Eventually he will forget you. There must be loads of girls at the school he is attending. Forget him. All men end up being monsters. Take it from me, no matter how good they may seem at first, or even if you marry them from the church and they profess to be Christians, they all end up being monsters, just like your father. Forget Jayce."

*****

" That is one of my favorite songs," Jayce said beside her.

Abigail opened her eyes, startled. She hadn't realized that he had come into the house or that he was sitting close to her on the carpet.

"I got that," she said huskily, "it is the only song on the CD." She looked him over. He was in khaki pants and was wearing a blue shirt. He looked fit and handsome and so familiar that for a moment she felt lightheaded with thankfulness that he was still in her life. Her mother's admonition to forget him had not quite worked out, had it? And by no stretch of the imagination was he a monster. Not now or then.

"You look spooked," Jayce said slowly. "Is everything okay?"

"I am fine." She nodded and looked into the box. "Just

unpacking your records…had a little break, that's all." She had gotten sucked into the memories that she had tried for years to bury.

For years she had tried to forget that night. She had escaped to Kingston but not from that beating. She was hospitalized when she had started vomiting blood. For weeks, she had been at the mercy of nurses and doctors. She was bleeding internally from blunt force trauma. Her father had almost killed her, and all in the name of punishment.

"This is the last of the boxes," Jayce said, pointing to the one beside him.

"It says *Haley*." Abigail looked at the side of the box.

"It does?" Jayce groaned. "Darn Melody and her efficiency. She must have looked in there and labeled it for me. She helped me pack up my apartment after I got shot."

"You still keep stuff from Haley?" Abigail asked softly.

"Yes. I am sorry you had to see this." Jayce picked up the box again.

"No, wait!" Abigail said. "I want to see what's in there."

"No, you don't," Jayce said. "I am going to have a bonfire with this."

"You don't have to do that, Jayce," Abigail said, half-smiling. "It's not a bad thing that you still have keepsakes from a high school relationship. I think it's cute how loyal you still are to Haley's memory."

Jayce set down the box and frowned at Abigail. "Abby, what I felt for Haley wasn't cute. I heard what you said at the Natural Life Festival. How you had to change and that changing and letting go of the past is the only way to move on. Well, I think it is high time I do that as well. I like you, I seriously do, and parading Haley around at every opportunity is not right. It feels wrong and juvenile. How you can find it cute is beyond me."

"Did you ever find out where she is now?" Abigail asked hoarsely. She was filled with mixed emotions. She wanted to yell, *I am Haley,* but she couldn't; she knew she couldn't.

Jayce frowned. "I tried looking for her at first when I came back to Jamaica from college. My dad's business was just getting off the ground and I had to help more at the time and then I went to Miami one summer and saw her mom at a church convention eight years ago and I asked about Haley. She said that Haley is married and happy. Her dad told me a couple of weeks ago that she didn't keep in touch with them."

He shrugged. "That's understandable." He put his head in his hands. "You know what the worst part about breaking it off with Haley was?"

"What?" Abigail asked softly.

"We never said goodbye."

"Like with your mom?" Abigail touched his hand.

"Yes. No closure," Jayce said, looking at Abigail. "It hurt like hell. It would have been better if we had a fight, or I met somebody else or something. She just disappeared. I think that's the reason she is so prominent in my head...that, and the fact that we share the same birthday. So every year, I remember, then it takes about half a year to forget and then when I am doing okay again...it's our birthday."

*****

After Abby left, Jayce sat in his partially-arranged living room. He lay on the couch, looking up at the ceiling. After talking about Haley again tonight, he realized that he needed closure—at least to look her in the face and have her tell him what happened to her and why she left without saying anything to him.

He understood her leaving her father but not him, never him. Even though he had resigned himself to moving on, he had only been paying lip service to it. He may not even have a pigeon's heart, as his father had insisted. He might be one of those people who just couldn't move on without a proper goodbye. But his mother had left and it hadn't affected him as badly. He had survived but maybe because his dad filled the gap and he was young when she left.

He grappled for his cell phone in the darkness. He wanted to know where Haley was. He owed it to himself to say goodbye.

Chapter Eleven

"**J**ayce." His father stood at his office door with his arms folded and a concerned look on his face. "I knocked on your door this morning. You didn't answer."

Jayce looked up at his father. "Dad, today is a rest day. I took the opportunity to sleep in late. I fell asleep on my couch last night. My house is finally livable and looking good, too."

His father glowered. "I didn't declare today a rest day."

"Yes, you did," Jayce said. "Last week you said I can get Wednesdays off. 'Five days of the week are enough to exercise.' You even threw in a compliment that I was doing better. Forgot that conversation?"

His father entered his office and closed the door behind him. He sat in the chair across from Jayce and cleared his throat. "That girl, Rashida, has been calling me non-stop since the Festival. She invited herself to run with me this morning."

Jayce chuckled. "And..."

"Jayce, she knows where I live and work and she has been sauntering past my office at odd hours of the day, and this morning she showed up at my house. She was waiting at the gate when I got out. She is stalking me."

"She is?" Jayce wriggled his brows. "And a big, bad general like you is afraid of her?"

His father scowled. "I am sixty; she is what, twenty-one? This is ridiculous. She could be my granddaughter."

"That's a stretch," Jayce snorted.

The General fanned him off. "Besides, I don't do office dating, nor do I think it is seemly to consort with the younger members of staff."

Jayce leaned back in his chair and steepled his fingers. "What a conundrum, General. Whatever will you do now?"

"How are things with you and Abigail?" The General asked.

"Fine," Jayce said. "I am slowly getting to know her. Did I tell you I think she is a mind reader?"

"No you didn't, but that sounds ominous, real bad." The General cleared his throat impatiently. "Please take Rashida off my hands. Pretend you like her. Date her for me. Keep her busy and occupied. You are closer to her age."

"No." Jayce laughed. "Begging me to take a girl off your hands is beneath you, General. She's too young for me, not just in age; she acts young, and besides, she looks like she is only interested in you, boss."

The General groaned. "I hate being harsh to the young ones. I don't want to break her spirit. She's so chirpy."

Jayce grinned. "Isn't she?"

The General got up. "By the way, got a call from Senator Oliver Hillman. He and I go way back. I was telling him that you were designing a voice-enabled home automation and security system that can do *Star Trek* stuff and he was excited. So excited in fact that he wanted it installed at his mansion in Rose Hall."

"Dad!" Jayce said, exasperated. "Xavier and I are not even done with the thing yet. I have yet to install it on my house to test it."

"What's taking so long?" The General frowned. "Didn't you say you installed it at Xavier's?"

"I did," Jayce said, "but there are a few bugs to work out. I just finished working on them. I am going to install it on my house and then see if everything runs smoothly. And only then will I even think of installing it on someone else's house, and certainly not a paying customer."

"You have two weeks to work out all the kinks. Oliver needs it to work," The General said unreasonably. "Apparently Oliver is scared for his life. Somebody killed his secretary last month and his confidant and chief companion, Hunter, mysteriously died this week. Oliver says he suspects poison. The people around him and connected to him are dying mysteriously; he assumes there is a vendetta against him. He is scared for his life and the poor thing was recently diagnosed with lung cancer."

"So offer him our comprehensive security package," Jayce said.

"I did. He is moving to his new place next week—said he desperately needs a break from Kingston—but after I told him about your system, he said he wanted it, along with our comprehensive security package."

"You shouldn't have told him," Jayce said. "Why are you so impatient?"

"It's business, Jayce. You are sitting on a gold mine and you are here slowly caressing it and cherishing it like a toy. I know," The General snapped his fingers. "Aren't you having a housewarming party? I will invite him so you can show off the technology."

"To my house? No!" Jayce sputtered, "I wasn't even thinking of having a housewarming party. Besides, he is your friend. If I had a party, it would be with my friends and you, of course, and a pastor to do the prayer…one that I like. Definitely not Greenwald. I don't want him anywhere near my home. I wonder if Bobby James can make it to the housewarming?"

"I thought you said you weren't having one," The General said skeptically.

"I wasn't but it is a great idea." Jayce nodded. "Thanks."

"Install the system and invite Hillman. He'll be my plus one."

Jayce shrugged. "We'll see."

The General got up. "Do it."

When he left, Jayce called Let's Party. Cynth answered. "Jayce," she said warmly when he identified himself. "It took you two whole months to finally decide to shake off the immature girls who are pursuing you and get in touch with a real woman."

Jayce chuckled. "Actually Cynth, I was wondering if you guys can fit me in a week before Christmas. Housewarming party."

"Are you sure you weren't calling to ask me out on a date?" Cynth asked.

"Yes Cynth. I am sure."

"Well…your loss, because I would make a wonderful wife."

Jayce chuckled. "I am sure you will make a wonderful wife to a very understanding man."

Cynth laughed. "A week before Christmas is the killer week but Ruby will insist that you are family so…" He heard shuffling. "Would the 19th be okay for you? It is our only free evening for all of December."

"Sure," Jayce said. "My secretary will send over the names and numbers of the invitees and anything else you need."

"Okay, handsome," Cynth purred. "Was there anything else you wanted me to do?"

"I want you to be good and take care." Jayce laughed and hung up the phone.

Next he called Abigail. They had to have a working lunch.

*****

Abigail walked into the office at lunchtime with the delivered food. "Why is everyone so busy?" She cleared a part of Jayce's cluttered desk and put down the containers with the take-out burgers. "It's like there is a burning building somewhere."

"Everyone wants security at this time of the year. Large and small companies beef up security, so we have to offer manpower and technological assistance and you name it."

He admired her as she bit into a burger. She was in a maroon polo shirt with the Owl Security logo and jeans. He looked at her and wondered if she knew just how distracting she was in jeans.

"What?" Abigail asked. "Aren't you going to eat?"

"Oh." Jayce looked down at his burger. "Not really feeling hungry. Do you realize how absolutely gorgeous you are?"

Abigail stopped chewing and lowered her burger to her lap. "Thank you."

"You have sauce right there." Jayce reached across the desk and wiped it away, tracing the outline of her lips.

Abigail closed her eyes and whispered, "Stop."

"But why?" Jayce withdrew his hand. "Your lips are like a

scarlet ribbon; your mouth is lovely."

Abigail giggled. "Songs of Solomon 4:3. You used to..." She cleared her throat loudly. She almost slipped and said, "You used to quote Songs of Solomon to me all the time." Luckily, Jayce's cell phone rang at the same time and he answered it.

"Yes, Norman. You found her. Great. Yes. Send over the report. Thanks."

He hung up the phone, a distant look in his eyes. "So I took your advice."

"My advice?" Abigail asked, alarmed. "When did I give you advice? What did I say?"

"You said that you loved the song *Natural Mystic* because it told you that you had to change, you can't bring back the past, et cetera. I thought about it last night and I think that I haven't moved on all these years because I never got the chance to say goodbye to Haley. So I asked somebody to track her down for me. I am going to put the past behind me once and for all. I can't change it but I can work with what is now."

Abigail gasped. "You what?"

"Tracked her down," Jayce said. "I am going to find her and get closure. I should have done it a long time ago. Instead, I used food as a crutch. You know, started the whole emotional eating thing and got so big that I lost self-confidence— convinced myself that I couldn't like anybody else and had a pigeon's heart but obviously that wasn't true because here you are. I like you and I have to stop bringing up Haley when I am around you. So I am going to give myself closure."

Abigail slowly put her half-eaten burger back in the wrapper. Her appetite had fled. "But... But I..."

"Don't worry about it," Jayce said. "I am not going to take one look at Haley and want to go back to where we were. You know what? Let's speak of happier things, like my housewarming party."

Abigail was staring at Jayce, semi-paralyzed. What kind of report would he have on Haley Greenwald? He had said that they could find out things that were not available to the regular public. She bit her lip in consternation. *What will he find?*

"Abby, over here," Jayce said, waving with a smile. "You are just looking fixedly at the corner."

"Oh yes." Abigail dragged herself from her panicked inner musings. "You said we were going to discuss your party."

"My father forced me into it," Jayce said, "because of business. He wants to invite his friend and I need to show him the technology I've been working on. Anyway, I was thinking of keeping it by the pool, and I am only inviting those near and dear to me—and my dad's friend, of course. I don't want a whole bunch of strangers cluttering my backyard."

Abigail smiled. "So you want me to arrange it?"

"No," Jayce said, "I already asked Let's Party to do it. You can just send over the names of the persons I am going to invite. They'll handle everything else. Are you going to eat first?" He looked at the burger.

"No, no," Abigail said, "I think I'll write first. I thought I was hungry. Turns out that like you, I am not as hungry as I thought."

"Okay," Jayce said. "I am doing this off the top of my head. I don't have that many friends... First invitee, Abigail Petri."

Abigail smiled. "You are inviting me to your party."

"But of course." Jayce smiled. "You decorated the place; you are my secretary and almost my girlfriend. And I love..." he paused. He was going to say he loved her, and he meant it, he did. He loved her though she was mysterious and uncommunicative about her past and exasperating and...

Abigail was staring at him with a stillness about her, and then he realized he couldn't declare his love for her like this. He would be a fool to do so now. He didn't want to feel her rejection and hear her explanations of why he was being foolish and sentimental.

"Love working with you," he said, correcting himself swiftly.

Abigail raised an eyebrow at him.

"Second and third on the list, my dad and his friend, Senator Oliver Hillman."

Abigail lowered the paper slowly. "Erm... who?"

"Oliver Hillman," Jayce said, tapping his cheek. "You have seen him on television, haven't you? He's one of the popular politicians—for foreign affairs, quite close to the prime minister too. He is moving to Mobay permanently and he is using us for his security needs."

Abigail's hands started to tremble. The shaking started somewhere in her spinal area and then spread out to her extremities, and despite the AC she felt a wave of heat overpowering her.

Oliver Hillman. Her ex-husband was moving to Mobay? Was his henchman Hunter moving here as well? But of course he was; Oliver did nothing without Hunter. They were as thick as thieves, and that was just one of their mutual sins, murder being another.

She almost missed the rest of names that Jayce called. It was a good thing that he wasn't looking at her intently, or he would have seen the goose bumps that were puckering on her arms.

"How many is that?" Jayce asked after a long enough list while she shakily wrote each name. She would have to go to her desk, hyperventilate a bit and then decipher what she had scribbled.

Abigail slowly counted the names on the list and had to start over three times. Her mind was in turmoil.

"You can be my point man on this, okay?" Jayce said, looking at his computer screen and becoming distracted by what was on it.

"Yes, fine." Abigail stood up.

Jayce grunted in response.

Abigail gathered the untouched burgers. *So much for a working lunch.* She left the room on shaky legs and deposited the food in her trashcan.

So Jayce was going to find closure with Haley and her ex-husband was in town. If only she could dump her stupid past and wipe her slate clean as easily as she did the burgers.

If only she could really be Abigail Petri, the independent girl who came from a loving family, who was married to her high school sweetheart and had two point five kids…if only she could be that completely fabricated girl, but she wasn't. Inside her, in her memories and life experiences was Haley Greenwald.

She sat down hard in her chair and took a deep breath.

Chapter Twelve

Jayce eagerly opened the file marked Haley Greenwald that he found in his mail. His contacts were usually thorough and quick. He didn't even watch Abby as she walked from the office, something which he always found pleasure in doing, no matter how busy he was. He was too engrossed in what he would find about Haley.

He almost found himself getting nervous, like a schoolboy just about to behold the forbidden. He remembered when Ian had found a gentleman's magazine in a teacher's desk in high school, obviously confiscated from a student and forgotten, and how they had gathered around the forbidden material, almost salivating to see what the big deal was.

He felt the same way now, jittery with anticipation. He clicked the link and his eyes ran over the information at a frantic speed.

"Haley Greenwald, changed her name to Haley Clarkson, her mother's maiden name, when she left Montego Bay.

She llived with Yvonne Clarkson and was hospitalized for broken ribs." He inhaled shakily; the date was two days after he left for school that January. *Had she hurt herself?*

He stopped his musing and continued reading. "Went to community college, did hospitality management for three years, and worked for Hillman International for six months.

His breath stopped when he saw the name Hillman. Oliver Hillman. "Married Oliver Hillman; became Haley Hillman."

His Haley had been married to his father's friend? The age gap was almost repulsive. Wasn't Hillman close to eighty? Was she still married to him? Was he going to meet Haley face to face in a short while? The thought almost scared him. Just then, his eyes picked up the words, "Haley Hillman, deceased."

His heart stopped beating. He was sure he wasn't breathing.

"No," he moaned as the words on the screen started running together in a blurry muddle. "Car crash." He looked at the date—four years ago.

He put his hand in his head, an irrational urge to cry overtaking him. *Haley was dead.*

How could it be that he hadn't been aware that she was no longer in the land of the living? How come something didn't alert him? He had loved her so much that he thought that...

He groaned, the sound escaping his lips before he could stop it.

"Jayce, is everything all right?" Abigail looked at him with concern from the doorway.

"Huh?" Jayce asked.

"You made a sound." Abigail frowned at him. "Like a wounded animal or something."

"Haley is dead," Jayce said flatly. His eyes were stinging. He didn't want Abigail to see him like this. He got up. "I am going to take the rest of the day off."

He inhaled roughly.

Abigail looked at him with sympathy. "Jayce..."

"I will be fine," Jayce said huskily. "I am just a little shocked right now. I just need time." He grabbed his car keys from the desk and headed through the door. He felt so down he could barely swallow past the lump in his throat.

When he reached outside building his footsteps faltered. It was raining. He stood in the downpour for what felt like hours. When he got into his car, he realized that he was wet and his eyes were blood red.

*****

"Jayce, seriously," Logan said impatiently, "I don't get it. It's been one whole week since you found out about Haley's death. You've been moping around the place like a dark specter. You missed practice last week."

"I had to convince him to come by today," Melody said. "It's a mystery why he is taking it so hard; Haley was fourteen years ago. There is a new person in your life. I can understand taking a day of coming to grips with your loss but a whole week?" Melody shook her head. "Pathetic."

"Leave him alone to grieve," Carson said sympathetically. "At least this time he is working out instead of eating obsessively like the last time she left him."

"And it shows," Ruby piped up. "You are looking really good, Jay."

Jayce grunted. "Thanks, I guess. I can't have my closure now and it sucks. I suck. The world sucks. Practice sucks. You guys suck."

"Fourteen years and you still want closure?" Melody closed her laptop. "You are one unique man. I pity Abigail. Don't let this interfere with your here and now, Jayce. You have always searched for reasons to alienate women from your life. Don't let this one slip away, you hear me!" She got up. "Have a good practice, guys."

Ruby got up too. "For your party, Jayce, I contacted Bobby James. He can't make it. Are you sure that you don't want Greenwald?"

"Absolutely sure," Jayce snarled. "That man was a terrible father. You know, I asked him about Haley and he said he didn't know where she was. Bet he doesn't know that she is dead, and he is sitting around in self-righteous confidence that she will come back when she is reformed. He doesn't even know that his daughter is dead."

Ruby raised her eyebrows. "Okay, so no Greenwald then. Let's see. Do you like Pastor Forbes? Would you mind him filling in for the blessing?"

"Fine." Jayce shrugged. "Right now, I am not caring. I don't need a pastor. Carson can do the blessing."

Ruby quirked her brow and looked at Carson, who nodded.

"Okay, then. I'll need to see the space I am working with."

"Abigail will show you around," Jayce said. "Just call the office."

Ruby smiled. "Okay, cool. I'll get to meet Abigail. She must be a paragon of virtue, sitting around and watching you feeling down about a woman you haven't seen in fourteen years. I have to do some damage control for you."

When she left the guys were silent until Ian said, "You have got to stop acting like this if you like Abigail, and if you are as serious about her as you say you are."

"Is she a Christian?" Carson asked, rubbing his chin. "I mean, what sort of relationship does she have with God?"

"No, better yet," Ian asked, "is she the loyal, honest type of person? And does she really like you?"

"I think if Jayce likes her there must be some good qualities there," Aaron said. "She seemed like a very nice person when we met her at the Natural Life festival."

"Oh, she likes him," Xavier said in reply to Ian. "When we saw her at the restaurant she couldn't take her eyes off him and here he is screwing it up with his Haley obsession. Haley is dead. Move on."

"That's cold," Jayce said and then it dawned on him suddenly, while the guys were talking that Abigail had practically pre-empted this conversation. It made him feel strange.

He looked at Logan. He hadn't said anything about her yet. Would he ask if she read? That's what Abigail had said he would say.

He waited in anticipation for Logan to speak.

Logan raised his eyebrows. "What? You want my opinion on Abigail? She looks good physically. The questions are, is she intelligent, and can she hold a good conversation and does she read because let me tell you..."

Jayce started laughing.

"What?" Everybody asked, looking at Jayce strangely.

"You won't believe this," Jayce said, "and this may spook you, but Abigail said exactly the same thing about you guys. Every one of you...your response to meeting her. It was eerily accurate. At the time I felt weirded out by it."

"She did?" Logan asked.

"Yes." Jayce nodded, and then he frowned. "She did. Are you sure that you have never met her before? He looked at the guys. "Think."

"Nope," Carson said. "I would remember if I had."

"She did seem familiar to me," Xavier said, "but then again, I think it was more of a feeling, not an actual meeting her kind of thing. Sorry."

"You know what I like about her?" Ian said. "She will help

you get over this Haley depression. I only hope she sticks around while you grieve."

"I understand his grief," Aaron said. "I liked Haley; she was my friend too. She was funny and outgoing and extremely kind and jovial. You remember, guys. She and Jayce complemented each other. We always thought that you two would get married before Carson and Alice."

"She was a friend to all of us and yes she was great," Logan said, "but life went on, she left without telling any of us goodbye. That showed that she wanted us out of her life and you know what, there is nothing wrong with that; life has a way of going that way. As Jayce said, she went to school, got married to that old geezer Oliver Hillman, and didn't look back. It is pointless to have a Haley memorial; she might not have even remembered us. Are we going to practice or what? Tomorrow I will start working at my big case with a new paralegal."

"What happened to the old one?" Ian asked.

"Food poisoning," Logan grimaced, "so I am getting a replacement from the agency. I hate temps, especially in the middle of a case. Argh." He groaned. "And my temp's name is Barbie. I kid you not. That's her legal name. It's not short for Barbara or even barbwire. Even the doll had a full name but no, my temp's actual name is Barbie."

Even Jayce was roused out of his despondency to have a chuckle at that.

"She probably looks like a doll," Carson said.

"Probably," Logan shrugged. "If she can't do the work, though, I am sending Barbie back."

Chapter Thirteen

Abigail waited patiently at Jayce's gate for Ruby. She had taken the afternoon to show Ruby around the house for the party. Jayce hadn't minded. He didn't mind many things these days since he found out that Haley died.

It made her feel guilty and mean and totally helpless to see him looking so miserable over her own staged death. She drummed her fingers on the steering wheel. Jayce had handed her his car keys silently. It was as if he was barely existing.

Ruby drove up and blew her horn. When she got out of the car, she smiled and waved to Abigail.

"It's lovely to meet you, Abigail," Ruby said briskly. "I haven't been here since Jayce bought the place. I've been extremely busy with Mommy duties and all that."

Abigail smiled politely. "How is that going?"

"Great!" Ruby said. "I love every single moment of every single day with my baby girl. I would have brought her with me now but my mom is in town."

Abigail showed her around, and they were standing by the pool area when Ruby looked at her admiringly. "You really know how to decorate a place. I mean, you have good taste."

"Thanks." Abigail shrugged. "I have always had a thing for design."

"Do you have a thing for Jayce?" Ruby asked slyly. "Because I know he has a thing for you."

Abigail shrugged. "He's cool."

Ruby looked deflated. "So you don't like him?"

"I do." Abigail frowned. "Why?"

"Well, he has been slumping around the place since he found out that Haley died. I hope that's not a turn-off for you," Ruby said quickly. "Please, don't worry about it. I can assure you this will pass. Jayce is a bit more complicated than others in the way he handles emotions. He is a nice guy—a real catch. I mean, even this grieving thing, when it passes will show you that Jayce is totally committed and loyal and caring and..."

Abigail laughed. "Sold. I get it. I have been working with him for the past two months. I know he is a total package."

"And he likes you," Ruby said, still in salesman mode. "You know, I kind of understand how he feels."

"You do?" Abigail asked interestedly.

"Yes, I do." Ruby sat down on one of the lounge chairs and indicated to Abigail to sit beside her. When Abby sat down she said wistfully, "I had a relationship before Ian. Great guy, but circumstances tore us apart and somewhere along the line we married other people, and then he came back into my life as the pastor of my church. To cut a long story short, it wasn't easy dealing with the residual feelings that we hadn't dealt with from back in the day, and now Jayce will never get that chance to with Haley. By the way, you should come by to Cedar Hill. Hasn't Jayce invited you yet?"

Abigail nodded. "He has. I tell him no every time. I go to a different church...Bramwell. It's walking distance from where I live; besides, I don't really want to meet your pastor and his wife."

"Oh," Ruby said interestedly. "You know Pastor Greenwald?"

Abigail nodded. "Yes. He's a huge man with an even bigger voice, isn't he?"

Ruby nodded. "Ironically, he's Haley's father, or should I say was." Ruby stretched and sighed. "Sister Greenwald had not come to join him in Jamaica for close to a year but now she is here. It was a rumored that they had split up, but I try not to listen to rumors. Most times they are wrong. The first lady is here now and she is a lovely lady. She teaches the tiny tots and the kids love her."

Ruby frowned. "It's weird, you know, nobody has ever heard the pastor or the first lady talk about their children or grandchildren. Pastor Greenwald is well loved at the church. He's a fire and brimstone and strict living kind of guy. He and the first lady complement each other well.

"Some persons say he is the best thing that has ever happened to the congregation. He rules with an iron fist. He hates the Band, though. Especially Jayce. No wait, I shouldn't say hate, but there is some strong animosity there."

Abigail was hanging onto Ruby's every word; that shocked Abigail. She had avoided all talk about her family so far, but had been quite stunned earlier this year when she heard that her father was the main pastor for Cedar Hill. It was as if circumstances were conspiring to bring the players from her past life together: her ex-husband, her father, and Jayce.

Abigail was having none of it. Haley was dead and would stay that way. She couldn't resurrect her now. She was safer living on the outskirts of all their lives.

Except that she really wasn't living on the outskirts, was she? She was sitting in Jayce's backyard, having a chat about her family and her old church with Ian's wife. That was more involved than she had bargained for.

Over the years, she had successfully tried to wipe her family from her mind. It had been remarkably easy to do, easier than wiping Jayce or her friends from her mind. After her aunt died, eight years ago, she had been effectively cut off from all familial contact and she had forced herself not to care.

While Ruby ruminated about her church and its merits, Abby thought about seeing her father face to face again. The last time she saw him he was full of wrath and raining blows all over her body.

For years after that, she had dreamed of exacting revenge on him. It had fueled her through college. It was because of him that she had married Oliver Hillman, the older businessman who had promised to fulfill all her material dreams. She had wanted to one day rub her father's face in it. She had wanted him to see that she had made it in the world.

The old feelings of bitterness rose to the fore again and she gasped when Ruby gently shook her. She blinked owlishly and focused on Ruby's concerned face.

"You were gone far, like you were in a trance," Ruby said, miffed. "I can't believe I was so boring."

"No, it's not you," Abigail said hoarsely and then cleared her throat. "I was thinking about my family. I was a pastor's kid and I was reminiscing about the bad old days."

"You were a PK?" Ruby grinned. "Is it true that pastor's children are the worst?"

Abigail chuckled. "I don't know about being the worst. I do know that they are the most ogled. Living life from the front pew isn't easy. Living life at home isn't easy either, especially if your father is an avid perfectionist with other, older children who were not very exemplary."

"Ah," Ruby looked mollified that Abigail had not found her boring and she was settling back in her chair for more information.

Abigail groaned inwardly. She wanted to be friends with Ruby; she was easy to talk to and seemed like a genuinely nice person. She had offered her a snippet about her life and now she had to share even more. That was the issue with making friends. They expected information and communication. Communication would lead to trust and the next thing she would be letting down her guard and spilling her secrets.

She regretted giving Ruby the info she already had, and fretted that she would tell Jayce. She didn't want him putting any information about her together. Haley needed to rest in peace. Her feelings of bitterness toward her family needed to rest in peace. She had buried them; where this sudden onset of bitterness and anger came from, she didn't know.

Maybe it was when Ruby said the children at church loved her mother that a little part of her had melted. Her mother had been a good mother to her when she was a little girl. Something happened along the way to her, though.

Little by little, year by year, after her eldest sister left home, she became a shadow of her former self. She became meeker and weaker while her father became sterner and stronger.

Her mother had also been the one who told her to forget the family and move on with her life. Her mother had not contacted her when she had stayed with her aunt. She could imagine that her father would not care if she was dead or alive but her mother was another matter.

Her head started throbbing the pain sneaking its way over her left eye. "I am going to take a tablet," she said to Ruby faintly. "I have a headache."

"Poor you," Ruby said, picking up her stuff. "I have to go. I have a party in two hours. Will you be all right?"

"Sure," Abigail said. "I just need to sleep this off." She needed a dark place and place to rest from the myriad of thoughts and emotions that were pelting her.

She went to one of Jayce's guest rooms. She had decorated the room in different shades of blue. She hurriedly drew the blinds, took two tablets for her headache, and stretched out on the bed. It felt so good to be on a proper bed, one that didn't have a wide sink in the middle.

She closed her eyes. The room was so quiet she could hear her own breathing. This was bliss, solitude, peace. The corrosive emotions that she had earlier dissipated and she drifted off to sleep.

*****

"Hey," Jayce said softly.

"Hey," Abigail blinked, coming awake fully. The side lamps were on and the room was bathed in light. Jayce was sitting beside her on the bed, propped up on the headboard and leafing through a large textbook with what looked like computer codes on the front.

"Oh my," Abby groaned. "What time is it?" Her belly rumbled at the same time.

"Nine o'clock," Jayce replied. "You snore. It's cute. Not like a big truck pulling up at the station kind of snore but little snuffling sounds."

Abigail grimaced and sat up. "I had a monster headache. I am so sorry I didn't come back with your car."

"No problem. The General swung by to check out the decor and the new system. He gave me a lift here." Jayce chuckled when her belly rumbled again. "I can make a sandwich for you."

"Thanks," Abigail said, heading for the bathroom.

Jayce put down the book and got up. He suddenly felt free from the dark, depressing thoughts that weighed him down all week.

It had been a comforting feeling to come home and find Abigail fast asleep in his guest room. He had like pottering around knowing that she was within physical reach.

He exhaled. It was time to join the land of the living; Haley was dead. He was alive.

*****

"I feel so embarrassed," Abigail said, sitting around the kitchen nook where Jayce had prepared a sandwich. "I was just going to take a nap and then come right back to the office."

Jayce inclined his head. "I know you fell asleep. I know you had a headache. The infrared biometric scanner from my security system had your neural response readings sky-high. I also know when you went to sleep, what time your headache went away, and when you started dreaming, though I am not sure if my brain wave technology is reliable."

"Wow." Abigail bit into her sandwich. "The technology can do all of that? There are no visible cameras anywhere."

"That's right," Jayce said smugly. "We use waves like your WiFi or cellular phone signals. You can't see it, can you?"

"No." Abigail shook her head.

"But it's here," Jayce said, "and it can read your heart and brain patterns. It's pretty amazing and it's working well. I checked in on you from the office on my phone. When I saw that you were sleeping I didn't bother to call.

"My Dad was so pleased when he saw the readings, because now that he knows how it works, we can hook up his friend Oliver, and he can have the peace which he was yearning for."

Jayce crossed his hands over his chest. "I don't understand what women see in Oliver. Why would a woman marry a man that is forty-two years older than her?"

Abigail's head snapped up. "Huh?"

"It's Haley." Jayce sat down on the stool across from her. "I know I bring her name up so much. but the whole thing is a puzzle to me. I have issues letting go of puzzles or anything remotely mysterious." He drummed his fingers on the table. "Haley was Oliver Hillman's ex-wife; that in itself is amazing. I must admit I have been mulling about that all week. It's such a small world. I mean, who knew that my Haley—I mean, Haley—had joined his harem?"

Abigail cleared her throat. "Maybe Haley was a gold digger. Oliver Hillman is rich."

Jayce shrugged. "It's possible but I just hate thinking about it. Almost as much as I hate thinking about her being dead."

Abigail finished her sandwich and got up. "Maybe her husband killed her."

"Why?" Jayce asked, frowning. He was looking at her interestedly.

Abigail pulled open the fridge. "Well, how old was Haley when she married this old dude?"

"Twenty-four according to court records," Jayce said helpfully.

He was getting into the spirit of the guessing game. Abigail sighed. "So she was twenty-four. He was sixty-six and she was his fifth wife or something."

"Yes," Jayce said. "She was wife number five."

"And they divorced?" Abigail asked. "Why?"

She waited to hear if Jayce knew anything more. Obviously, he had been researching, but he just shrugged. "They divorced four years later. No explanation was given in the report I got."

"And that is the year she died," Abigail said. "Haley knew something. Oliver is an old guy in politics, and his companies are always getting huge contracts and what-not. He must have done some real shady stuff in his life. Maybe Haley found out about it, couldn't live with it, and instigated a divorce. Besides, she must have been reaching Oliver's sell-by date. Aren't all his wives like really young, nobody over thirty?"

Jayce was staring at her, transfixed. "That's right. I never thought of that. How'd you...never mind."

"And so he divorced your Haley but she knew too much, so old dude hired someone to kill her. A car accident would be a good cover."

"Oh my," Jayce said. "You are good at this." He laughed uncomfortably. "You almost had me believing that this is the real story."

"I can bet you, Jayce, that that is exactly how it went," Abigail said, unscrewing the bottle of water.

Jayce felt uneasy when she said that. She had eerily predicted, almost verbatim, what his friends would say about her, and now this.

Abigail was sipping from her water bottle and staring through the window at her reflection.

"Maybe that is why people around him are dying," Jayce said reflectively. "Maybe that's why he is fleeing Kingston and hiring our security firm. Maybe some of his bad deeds are coming home to roost. Someone killed his close friend and assistant, Hunter Newby. His secretary died last week. All of his trusted people are dying; maybe it started with

Haley. Maybe someone killed Haley thinking that they were getting back at him."

Abigail stopped swallowing and choked on her water. She sputtered and started coughing. "That's clever. How did you think of that?" she squeezed out of her suddenly clogged throat, but all she was thinking was that Hunter was dead. She hadn't expected that—one link to that side of her life gone.

"Well, well," Jayce said smugly, "it seems as if I am not the only one who can build a story." He went around to her side of the table and knocked her on the back. "Feel better now?"

"Yes," Abigail said, straightening up. "Thanks."

Jayce looked down in her eyes. He searched her face thoroughly. "I am sorry."

"For what?" Abigail asked uncomfortably.

"For being such an ass about this whole Haley thing. I was stupid." He traced the outline of her lips. "Because you are here with me now. I have moved on."

He lowered his head to hers and whispered, "I am going to kiss you, and this time when I kiss you, I will know that I am kissing Abigail Petri."

Abigail sucked in a deep, charged breath. He didn't touch her body, made no attempt to hold her; he just captured her lips and whispered, "Abby."

Chapter Fourteen

Abigail let herself into her apartment and locked the door. It was after one in the morning. After kissing Jayce, they had watched a movie, a historical epic that had her on the edge of her seat. Jayce had fallen asleep in the middle of it, though. She laughed softly. She knew that it was not his kind of movie, but he had valiantly watched the first twenty minutes with her.

She kicked off her shoes and clothes and stepped into the shower. The water pressure was low and she stood under the trickling water and stared sightlessly at her off-white tiles.

She had no hopes of sleeping now that she had practically slept out the day. She could spend all night right under the trickling water, just staring. She felt burdened by a heavy weight hanging over her. She always felt this way after discussing her past life as Haley, especially with Jayce. The whole situation was a little twisted.

In a bid to distance herself from Haley, she had called

herself a gold digger. She hadn't been, not really. She had been troubled and bitter and almost certifiably so by the time she had joined Hillman Inc.

She had been on the outs with God, totally blaming Him for the mess her life was in, though it wasn't her fault. She had lost everything: her parents, her friends, and Jayce, and she hadn't recovered. Forgetting wasn't as easy as her mother suggested that it was.

She had been lonely. She had turned twenty-four that October 5th; as usual, she bought herself a birthday cake and lit two candles on the thing: one for herself and the other for Jayce.

Her aunt Barbara had called her earlier sobbing that she had gone to the doctor and they had discovered that her cancer had spread, which made her birthday bittersweet and even more depressing than it usually was. Barbara was her only family link.

That day when Oliver Hillman saw her blowing out the candles in the company cafeteria, it was past lunchtime and she had made sure that no one was around. A tear or two had slipped from her eyes. Her future looked bleak, and she was upset over her aunt, and at that moment she had wanted to chuck it all in and return to Montego Bay.

She missed Jayce so much that she was aching from it. She didn't care that her parents wanted her gone and that her father almost killed her. She just wanted to escape her pathetic life. It just kept getting worse. There was not even a little break for her.

"What's a pretty girl like you doing crying over a cake?" Oliver asked, sitting down across from her.

He was old was the first thought that entered Haley's head, and he was the big boss. What was he doing in the cafeteria?

Oliver inclined his head. "Is it your birthday?"

"Yes sir." She nodded. "It is."

"No 'sir'," he said, chuckling. "Gosh, don't call me sir. I am Oliver or Ollie. My close friends call me Ollie. Want to be one?"

"One what?" Haley asked him, confused.

"Close friend." He leaned forward, his eyes twinkling. "I like you. What's your name?"

"Haley." She cleared her throat. "Haley Greenwald."

"Mmm." He licked his lips. It was obscene; his tongue had little black dots on it and it left traces of spittle at the corner of his mouth. She recoiled inside.

"Let me take you to dinner so you can celebrate your birthday properly."

"No," she shook her head, "I don't think so."

He looked taken aback; he had not expected rejection. "Why not? Have a boyfriend?"

"No." Haley shook her head vigorously and then blurted out involuntarily, "You are older than my father!"

Oliver chuckled and winked at her. "But I am not cold."

Haley had actually felt a little disturbed at his blatant flirting. Until now she had spurned any advances made to her by anyone, and Oliver Hillman would be the last man she would date. He was old and unattractive. His face had too much character to be called ugly but he was far from being attractive to her. As a matter of fact, he reminded her of a pig, with his squinty pale eyes and snout-looking nose and pinkish complexion.

He may not have been handsome but he was confident and extremely persistent. After that initial meeting, he had pursued her with a determination that had bordered on obsession. At the time she hadn't realized that her very repulsion of him was a turn-on to Oliver. He was used to getting things easily because of his millions. He had already been through four young wives and he had been actively hunting for a fifth.

When her aunt died five months after her first meeting with Oliver, he had been the only one to support her at the funeral. She had contacted her mother to tell her and Hannah Greenwald had actually pretended she didn't know her. She had muttered something unintelligible and hung up the phone on her. She had felt alone, isolated and grief stricken, with her only family link in the world gone. That was when Oliver had proposed.

Filled with grief and a deep desire to prove to her parents and the world that she didn't need anybody, she had married Oliver Hillman and she had well and truly left her past behind her. She had reinvented herself as the lady of the manor, Haley Hillman. All the time, though, she had been mindful that Oliver did not particularly like to keep his wives for long and she had quietly planned her exit strategy.

After witnessing him and Hunter cold-bloodedly killing someone, she had taken her head out of the clouds. She had requested a divorce. Her conscience, which she had thought had long since died, could not deal with what she saw. She couldn't pretend that all was well with her world anymore.

Oliver had gladly granted her the divorce. He realized his mistake in having her around when he killed one of his shady crime partners, but he couldn't have her running around with that knowledge.

He had recently been appointed a senator when the new government came to power, and he was a businessman, a well-respected pillar of society. Having her out in the world with her knowledge of him, like a loose canon, was not going to sit well with him.

He had to have her silenced. She realized that as soon as she moved out, and several attempts were made on her life. She was a target and she knew that Hunter, his chief henchman, was the one who was sent to do the deed.

She had gotten so desperate that she had gone to the police with her story. It was immediately squashed. The detective had taken her to a superintendent and he had laughed at her accusations, and quoted Shakespeare. "Hell hath no fury like a woman scorned, huh? Don't go making trouble for the senator."

Returning from the police station, she had been in an accident. A car had rammed into hers and sent her careening off the road and flying through the windshield. Her face had taken most of the impact.

She remembered waking up in a hospital. Her jawbone was broken and wired shut she couldn't speak. Her eyes were swollen and she could barely see through them. Hunter was standing over her with a fierce look in his eyes.

"I knew you weren't dead," he whispered over her harshly. "Listen to me." He was so near she could feel his breath on her skin.

She had seriously thought that he was about to finish the deed and had closed her eyes tightly.

"You've been in here four days." Hunter growled, "Are you hearing me?"

Haley opened her eyes and tried to plead with him not to kill her but she couldn't move her mouth.

"I hoped you had died after I rammed your car." He sighed, "I don't want to kill you. Every time I attempt to, I just can't, and there is this guy that has been following you around. He looks fierce. Who is he, your new security? I may not be able to kill you but Oliver insists that you must die."

He moved even closer to Haley's battered face. "I told him that you were dead. I have a friend that knows how to forge death certificates. You had better stay dead, you hear me?"

he said threateningly.

"I know a plastic surgeon that Oliver's second wife used; he's really good. Your face looks like hell now; you'll probably need him anyway. I am telling you this because I already called him. Don't let him restore your face to your previous one. Create a new identity and start your life again or else I will have to kill you, whether you have that guy following you around or not. I may have to kill him too. Disappear, you hear me?" he finished roughly.

Haley had swallowed and sighed with relief when he moved away. When he left, she had wondered if Hunter had gone mad or was seeing things. She didn't have any fierce security following her around. She wished she had thought of hiring one, but she hadn't. She had wanted to preserve her money, maybe invest in a business, so that she could have some income in the future.

The more she thought about what he said about the plastic surgery, the more she could see the sense in it. It was not the first time someone was telling her to disappear.

Her mother had told her to before, and now Oliver wanted her dead. She would be better off as somebody else. Maybe she should reinvent herself. That would be better for all concerned.

When she looked at her face in the mirror for the first time after the accident, she realized that she might not even have a choice. She looked like a massive purple bruise and only one of her eyes could be opened. One eye socket was broken, one jaw broken, and her nose was pulp. She had tried not to cry.

"What date is it?" she asked the surgeon who had come to her for a consultation.

"February 1," he said gently. "Are you sure that you don't want your old face back? He was looking at one of her pictures, which she had shown him on her phone. "I could do that, you know. You have such lovely bone structure."

"Yes, I am sure," Haley murmured. "I don't want to look like the old me at all. Change me so that not even my parents will recognize me."

The doctor had nodded. "Okay." He had shown her several sketches after that. She had leafed through each one and decided on a new face.

Her stay in the private hospital had been a long one. Various church groups had come by. One church lady, Marie Petri, had taken it upon herself to personally visit Haley.

"What's your name?" she asked one day when Haley was lying in bed after her second rhinoplasty.

"I don't know," Haley whispered. "I am nobody."

"Oh no, you have amnesia," Marie said sympathetically, completely misunderstanding her. She really didn't know who she was. She hadn't thought of a name for herself.

"Don't worry about it," Marie said optimistically. "God knows your name, whoever you are. He loves you, he will take care of you, and he has a plan for you. You are alive today because of him."

Haley pondered that. Did God really love her? He must have because Oliver had wanted her dead and yet he had sent an angel to protect her, an angel that only Hunter had seen. Only God could have used the man who was sent to take her life to suggest to her that she needed a new identity.

She was seeing God in a different light these days and she realized that maybe He had orchestrated things to sort out her life. The thought made her less lonely and less sorry for herself.

Every day she looked forward to Marie's positive encouragement and one day when Marie was reading the Bible story of Abigail and how she intervened on behalf of her foolish husband, Haley decided that she was going to be

Abigail. She sounded like a good woman to emulate. She then searched her mind for a surname and then she thought that Marie's surname was good enough and was suitably rare. There couldn't be many Abigail Petri's in the world. That's when she became Abigail Petri.

She turned off the tap and toweled herself slowly. She was in a conundrum. She couldn't reveal her secret to Jayce now, not while Oliver Hillman was alive, and maybe not ever.

She shouldn't have returned to Montego Bay. She shouldn't have become involved in Jayce's life, but it was almost as if she couldn't help herself. She had wanted to come home.

Chapter Fifteen

Jayce's poolside party was in full swing before The General joined them with his friend, Oliver Hillman. The General had volunteered to show Oliver how the technology worked and they were in the house for the longest time, ruminating about their time together in the army. Oliver Hillman had been The General's superior when they were younger.

The poolside area was simply decorated with lanterns throwing off a green and yellow glow and mellow music wafting through the speakers strategically located outside.

Jayce had situated himself on a lounge chair that gave him a view of the entire pool area and especially Abigail. He couldn't take his eyes off her from the moment she had stepped into the house earlier. She had worn a simple pale pink dress and her hair was let loose in long, curly ringlets that flirted with her waist. She had on satiny makeup; her face was glowing.

She had been commandeered by the wives of his friends as

soon as she got in. He had barely said a word to her and now they were sitting in a circle at a stone bench laughing and talking with Abigail, every one of them trying to get to know her better, and she was enjoying their company. He could see that she had a grin on her face and sometimes she laughed out loud, usually at something Melody said. He wondered what tale about him Melody was spinning.

Jayce smiled. He didn't mind. He wanted her to like his friends. Now, more than ever, he wanted her to fit in because he was sure that she was the one for him. He watched as she laughed at something that Alice said. Even her pink lips were glistening, and then he saw her stiffen as her gaze strayed to the door. The cup she had in her hand shook perceptibly and she placed it on the stone table abruptly.

What could have caused such a reaction from her? He swiftly followed her gaze and saw that his father and Hillman had made their way to the pool area. Hillman looked relaxed and was laughing as The General was pointing around, obviously in his element.

He looked at Abigail again. Why would she look so uneasy to see his dad—or was it Hillman? Did she think that Hillman had really killed Haley? Now he felt sorry that he had brought up that speculation with her. Seeing Hillman had wiped the smile from her face and she was looking jittery.

He got up from the lounge chair and headed for her. His friends had monopolized her long enough.

"Hey," he bent down and whispered in her ear.

"Jayce's come for his girl," Melody said, grinning. "By the way, I like her." She gave Jayce a thumbs-up and the other ladies grinned and did the same.

Abby cleared her throat and got up. She was smiling as well, but it didn't reach her eyes.

Jayce tucked her hand in his. "What's wrong?"

"Nothing's wrong," Abigail said. "I like them, all of them. Alice is cool, Ruby is funny, Farrah is sophisticated, Alka is gentle, and Melody is nurturing..."

"I meant what's wrong with you?" Jayce stepped closer to a garden lamp and looked searchingly into her eyes.

"Nothing's wrong," Abigail insisted again, looking back at him with what she hoped was an innocent look.

"Remember what I said about you not lying so well?"

"Oh come on," Abby said. "Nothing's wrong. It's your house warming party; go spend time with your other guests."

Jayce frowned, ignoring her blatant attempt to get him to move away. "Was it the conversation that we had about Hillman that made you apprehensive when you saw him?"

"Oh God help us," Abigail groaned. "Do you watch my every reaction?"

"Yes," Jayce said unapologetically. "You communicate much better with your body than your mouth."

"I do?" Abigail snorted. "That's not true."

"Oh yes," Jayce said confidently. "I know you are attracted to me... really attracted, and you are fighting it. I don't know why you are fighting it but in case you don't know it yet, I have the hots for you too."

Abigail stifled a sigh. "Jayce..."

"I also know that Hillman spooked you. What I want to know is why?"

"It was nothing," Abigail said.

"Really?" Jayce looked at her long and hard. "So you won't mind if I introduce you two."

"Why would you want to?" Abigail asked. "I am not impressed by celebrities. I can cope without the introduction."

"Well it's out of your hands now; here he is with Dad," Jayce whispered. He was watching her keenly as they approached.

Abigail inhaled tremulously. Her hands were trembling; she used one to steady the other. She had not thought that she would behave this way, seeing Oliver again after nearly five years. Four years seven months and three days since the divorce.

She schooled her features into indifference. What was she reacting to, anyway? Oliver Hillman did not know her. She was Abigail Petri. She had a different face and a different name. She was a different girl; she had nothing to be afraid of.

The General, who was walking beside Oliver, grinned at the two of them. "Here is the man of the hour," his father said proudly. "New house and a new innovative working technology."

"Very impressive," Oliver said smoothly. He shook Jayce's hand. "And is this Mrs. Jayce?"

"Not yet," Jayce said, grinning. "I am working on it."

Hillman chuckled. "Nice to meet you, my dear." He held out his hand and Abigail wondered if she should shake it. She paused—not long enough for there to be any cause for alarm, but she saw the way that Jayce noticed her reluctance.

She took a deep breath and even managed to smile at the familiar face of her previous tormentor.

She shook his hand and hurriedly pulled her hands from his.

"I didn't get your name," Oliver said, giving her one of his probing looks. She knew that look. He had subjected her to it the first day they met. That was his hunting for a woman look—though the man was pushing eighty.

"Abigail," she replied huskily. She had to force herself to speak. Her voice had gone into hiding. She wished she hadn't come to the party. She was feeling a sudden onset of fear. It had belatedly dawned on her that this man could cause her serious problems if he found out who she was.

He was looking all jovial and civilized now but he was a cold-blooded killer and had a hit out on her life years ago because she knew what he had done. It was all good and well to think about him and the past with the distance of time and somehow diminish him in her mind, but he was right in front of her and her fears were crowding out her reasoning.

She dragged her eyes from Oliver Hillman's and swiveled to look at Jayce. She needed the reassurance of his presence right now.

He took one look at her and excused them both. She was not for the first time thankful that Jayce always seemed to read her, even when she didn't want him to. He knew she needed to escape.

She walked with him into the house, barely breathing when they reached the half dark living room; only a lamplight was on in the corner. Jayce sank into the settee with her held closely at his side. A panicked feeling of breathlessness had taken her over.

Jayce hugged her to him and rubbed her back silently, absorbing her tremors as she pressed her body into his.

Abby gradually came back to herself, the rush of sound in her ears subsided and she could once more hear the faint sounds of the music outside and the laughter and the chatter. She tried to straighten up but Jayce had her held so tightly against him she couldn't move.

"Talk to me," he said quietly.

"About what?" Abby said, regretting her breakdown even more now. She couldn't tell Jayce the truth.

Jayce whistled silently. "Abigail Petri, you just had a panic attack. What was that about?"

Abigail heaved a sigh. "Hillman reminds me of my ex-husband."

"He does?" Jayce twisted around in the settee and turned on the lamp on his side. "You were married to an old guy too?"

Abigail nodded abruptly. "Unfortunately."

"What's his name?" Jayce asked.

"I can't tell you," Abigail said, panic in her voice. "My ex-husband wants me dead, Jayce. I am sorry, okay. The less you know, the better."

"Okay, okay." Jayce gripped her hands. He wanted to ask her a million and one questions but he could see that she was getting agitated again.

"Look at me," he said softly.

Liquid brown, deep-set eyes stared at her. They were earnest and filled with compassion.

"I am here for you, always. Remember that."

"Thanks."

Jayce kissed her on her forehead.

"I think I should go," Abigail said. "I am not in the party mood."

"I'll drop you home," Jayce said quickly.

"No, I will call a cab." Abigail got up and fumbled in her bag for her cell phone. "It's not right for you to leave your own party."

Jayce grimaced. "You may be right. I hate that you have to leave though."

"There you are," The General said. Oliver Hillman was in his wake. "You know you will have to personally explain some things to Oliver. I am not as fluent in this technology as I had thought, and I want him to see the monitoring system in your office."

"Excuse him a moment, Abigail," The General said, pulling Jayce toward the home office and the bank of monitors he had in there.

Abigail was left standing in the living room with Oliver Hillman.

"So," Oliver Hillman said, rocking back on his heels. "How serious are you about Jayce?"

"Excuse me." Abby looked at him. She dialed the number for the taxi and wished that she had done so before now. It would take the taxi at least ten minutes to get to Jayce's house.

Until then she would be loitering around the place with nothing to do, maybe forced to small talk when she was not in the mood. She didn't want to answer any questions or be offered any sympathy; she just wanted to leave, especially now that she was alone with Oliver.

"How serious are you about Jayce?" Oliver asked again and winked at her when she came off the phone.

"He's my, er...friend," Abigail finished in a rush.

"Jayce and I seem to have the same taste in women," Hillman said, walking closer to her. "I learned recently that he was my ex-wife's childhood friend. Isn't that something?"

"Er...what?" Abigail asked faintly. Oliver Hillman was looking at her knowingly, as if he recognized her. How could this be? Her heart started thumping in earnest.

She looked nothing like Haley. She needed to remember that. She was Abigail, born on February 1, the day when she chose her new face, all because this man had ordered someone to kill her.

Oliver stood directly in front of her. "You remind me of someone."

Abigail laughed uncomfortably. "I do?"

"Yes," Oliver said, "you are a beautiful girl, my type of woman—want to ditch Jayce and move on with me? I have more money than I know what to do with and I have one foot in the grave. It would be nice if I could spend the last of my days with a young girl to keep me warm."

He coughed after that incredulous speech, and Abigail stared at him in horror. He was still an old Casanova and unrepentant with it, but he would not be coming on to her if he knew who she was, and that meant she had no cause for concern where he was concerned.

She relaxed slightly and almost smiled when he looked at her with watery eyes. "No thank you, Mr. Hillman. I quite like Jayce; he's more important to me than money."

*****

"Atta girl," The General said, smiling over the monitors. They had been watching the exchange after Jayce had turned on the monitors in the office and highlighted the living room.

"The sound on this is unbelievable," The General said.

Jayce breathed a sigh of relief after what Abigail said; for a brief moment he had been nervous as he watched her with Hillman.

"I can't believe that Hillman was propositioning my girl in my living room, knowing that I have security around. The old guy is something else, huh?"

"Maybe that's why he did it." The General shrugged. "But Abigail rebuffed him, which was a good thing because if she hadn't, I would have fired her tonight. Let's demonstrate this thing to him and get him out of here before he hits on any more of your friends."

Chapter Sixteen

"**W**hat are you doing this weekend?" Jayce asked Abigail casually. He had been biding his time all week after the party to ask her to go to church with him. The office was so busy and she had volunteered to assist his father's secretary with some of her work load, so he had hardly seen her and he wondered if it was deliberate. Whenever he felt as if he was getting closer to Abby she took a step back. It was tiring but he was seeing this through to the end.

He could see her rifling in her mind for an excuse not to come to church with him. Cedar Hill church seemed to give Abby the creeps. For the life of him, he couldn't fathom why.

"It's Alka's and Aaron's baby's blessing. I have your invite here." He patted his briefcase.

"No. Sorry. Can't make it," Abigail said. "I have other plans."

"What plans?" Jayce asked suspiciously. "It is a holiday weekend. You said you don't have any family alive. We usually have a whole host of things to do and we would love if you would join us."

"Who is this 'we'?" Abigail asked irritably. "I am not really into family stuff and friend stuff. This time of the year sucks."

Jayce nodded. "I see. You prefer to stay in your apartment and stare at the four walls. That sounds fascinating."

"I don't want to be included. I don't want to go to Cedar Hill church," Abigail said, getting up.

"You told Hillman that you preferred me over money," Jayce said when she turned to leave. "Seriously, as far as I am concerned that's a proclamation of love. You are officially my girlfriend or significant other, which means that you are going to spend the holiday with me. It's only the right and proper thing to do."

Abigail gasped. "You heard when I said that?"

"Yup." Jayce grinned. "I have been waiting to spring it on you all week."

Abigail shuddered. "I had to tell the old guy something; he was coming on to me. What I said didn't mean anything."

"Ha," Jayce said. "You meant it. You said every word with conviction. You like me more than you can say, and I am flattered. Truly I am."

"Dream on," Abigail said but her sharp retort lacked heat. She looked back at him, her hand on the door. "Your pastor, Greenwald, is he the one doing the blessing?"

"Yup," Jayce said, "Greenwald is the senior pastor. Lately he seems as if he has mellowed somewhat," Jayce said contemplatively. "Maybe it's because Sis Greenwald is here. You see, even the gruffest of men need a soft touch now and again."

Abigail stiffened. "How is she?"

"Who?" Jayce asked, puzzled.

Abigail bit her lip. Why would she be asking about Sister Greenwald? As far as Jayce was concerned, she shouldn't be curious.

"Alka," she settled on. "How is she?"

"Fine." Jayce grinned. "You saw her the other night. She is especially hopeful that you will come. There will be a dinner after, at Aaron's place. The family dinner is the week after so there will be friends and a few people from church."

Abigail's curiosity got the best of her. Though she wanted to see her parents, she had avoided the urge to do so. She didn't even know where they lived, and though she had vowed to completely remove them from her life, she was finding out that she was human after all. Just a glimpse of them would be fine with her.

"Okay. I will come."

"Great," Jayce said. "Excellent."

*****

The moment Abigail stepped through the doors of the Cedar Hill church she felt a sense of nostalgia so potent she closed her eyes for a brief moment to steady herself.

She had told Jayce that she would come by herself. She had all intentions of slipping into a pew at the back where she could observe the proceedings without being noticed but a young lady with a wide grin had greeted her at the door and said, "Hi, I am Mia. Uncle Jayce said I should watch out for you as soon as you got here and take you to him. He described you accurately."

Abby groaned. Mia had chuckled as if she understood her reluctance to go to the front of the church where she could see Jayce and his friends sitting.

Why did they have to sit at the front, all on one bench and

coupled up? She considered turning back toward the door and walking out but Mia was standing firmly behind her, not budging. She seemed as if she took the command from her Uncle Jayce seriously.

Abigail straightened her spine, tamped down her inclination to leave, and headed to the front.

Mia whispered, "Have a great day today."

She nodded and went to sit between Jayce and Alice. Both Alice and Jayce were smiling. She gave Alice a genuine smile and gritted her teeth at Jayce.

"You had to send your niece to get me?"

"Yup," Jayce whispered. "Because I knew you'd sit on the very last bench, hiding behind somebody's hat. I also told her that she should follow you if you attempted to go home."

Abigail resisted the temptation to roll her eyes. She gave him a half-smile instead. She was going to do all of the above; why argue?

She was in tune with the service until the platform party entered and she saw her father, Pastor Antonio Greenwald, in the flesh. It was the first time in fourteen years. She didn't realize that she was holding her breath until the congregation stood up and she was the only one left sitting.

She stood up abruptly, her eyes locked on him. He looked the same. He had a few more gray hairs, an extra bracket around his mouth, but his dark skin was smooth and otherwise wrinkle free, and he was still large. In the past he had a little bit of a paunch; it was now gone. He looked a tad slimmer. He looked better than he did when he was younger, or was it that she had imagined him as a monster for so long that she had skewed her picture of him in her mind?

He looked good for a sixty-two year old. She waited for the hate and resentment that she had toward him to show itself, but it never came.

She sat down when the rest of the congregation did, waiting for the bitterness to well up, but today she was curiously empty. She wasn't feeling particularly good or bad, just apathetic.

Before the sermon began, she whispered to Jayce, "Where's Sister Greenwald?"

"Children's church," Jayce said. "She loves kids."

"Okay," she whispered back. That was when her heart gave her a weird jab. Hannah Greenwald loved kids, just not her own, just not her.

She wondered where her sisters were now. The last time her curiosity had been piqued she had passed her older sister, Beatrice, in the supermarket. She had actually said hello and Beatrice had given her a kindly smile and said hello, with no recognition in her eyes. That was okay, Abigail had reassured herself then. The point of the surgery was that she wouldn't be recognizable to anyone who should know her.

That meeting had actually spurred her to visit the church where Beatrice was a first lady. Her husband was a popular television evangelist. She had found out that Beatrice had three children and was a teacher. She and her husband were unhappily muddling along with their relationship. There was talk of him having an affair and a child outside of wedlock but that was still unsubstantiated talk.

She half-listened while the song of meditation was going on, thinking about her other sister, Cher, who was no longer in the church. Cher was a broadcaster on a prominent local radio station and was very popular in the dancehall culture. She had married an entertainer in a very publicized wedding. It was her third marriage. So far, she had effectively turned her back on all things religious and nobody knew that her father was a minister of the gospel.

When her father got up to speak, Abby realized that

because of his attitude all three of his children were messed up to some degree—three girls and not one of them was close to him.

He had treated them like he was a general in an army. Ironically, Jayce's father, who was the real army man, treated his son with the kind of gentleness, attentiveness, and understanding with which one was supposed to treat a child.

The blame for their fractured family rested squarely on Antonio Greenwald's shoulders. He could easily lead the church flock but his family life was a complete mess. His gruff and stern way of handling children was wrong and his mode of discipline was more abusive than caring. Abigail wondered, not for the first time, what made him that way.

She wondered if he ever wished that things were different—if he ever tried to at least reconcile with Cher or even Beatrice, because he certainly hadn't tried with her. He couldn't swallow his pride or humble himself enough to say, *Sorry I was a lousy father*. Suddenly, she didn't want to hear his message. Her curiosity about him was assuaged. What could he legitimately tell her when she knew who he really was?

He was a proud man. The Lord did not work well with proud. In fact, that was the first of the seven things that God hated: a proud look.

She needed to hear her father say that he was sorry for the way he treated his children in the past—especially her. He had given her an uncalled-for beating that almost killed her.

She knew he felt that he was justified in punishing her that day and that was the scary part of all of this: her father thought that he was always right.

She closed her eyes briefly. It would take no less than God's intervention to change his heart. She whispered a prayer for him before he spoke, nonetheless.

Pastor Greenwald cleared his throat before starting to speak. "It is a good day to be alive, brethren."

There were a few amens at that statement.

"Today I realized how grateful we should be for life." He looked in the audience contemplatively. "Today I realized how utterly blessed we are for being here."

He opened his Bible. "The Holy Spirit prompted me to preach this sermon today. I don't know why," he said gruffly. "It's the story of Abigail. Nothing much is known of her background and her story is just a few lines in the Bible, but the Lord told me this morning that I should speak about Abigail. He said it, so I am doing it."

"That's you, Abigail." Jayce whispered to her. "Nobody knows much about your background."

Abby looked at him and smiled. "Shut up." Her mind was racing, though. God knew her secret; he knew everything. What if he told her father? Was his message coincidence? Just when she visited his church?

"The Bible describes her as beautiful and intelligent. Listen, not many women in the Bible are called beautiful and intelligent." Greenwald cleared his throat. "I appreciate women, and beautiful and intelligent in the same package... that's a good woman to have."

The church chuckled.

Jayce nodded beside her. "Definitely you, Abby."

"I have three girls. I know I don't talk about them much."

"He has two girls," Jayce mumbled under his breath. "Poor guy doesn't know that one is dead."

Abigail sat forward in her seat, barely breathing. She waited to hear more from her father.

Greenwald cleared his throat. "While I was drawn to this passage, 1 Samuel 25, I realized that Abigail means the father's joy. Every one of my girls was a joy to me. I wish

I could have named one of them Abigail. However, it's too late..." he chuckled. "Way too late. Sister Greenwald and I have passed that stage but if we were to do it again, we would do it differently."

His voice broke. "Much differently. As parents you live and you learn."

Abigail gasped. That was what her chosen name meant, 'father's joy'? If she had known she wouldn't have chosen it, and what was he talking about? He didn't love any of his girls, and he wanted a do-over? That was a public declaration from Antonio Greenwald that he was not the perfect father.

She felt flushed and her skin felt prickly.

"So, the story is an interesting one," Pastor Greenwald continued after his rumination. "Samuel, the great prophet of Israel, had just died and David, heir apparent to the throne, was running from Saul, the current king, who was hunting him down.

"David and his men took refuge in the wilderness of Paran, near Carmel. This is also where the wealthy man, Nabal, was pasturing his flocks of sheep and goats. Thanks to David and his men, Nabal's flocks and herds were well protected. Ironically, Nabal's name means fool, and he lived up to the name. At shearing time there was usually a big celebration and David sent to ask Nabal if his men could participate. Nabal gave David a foolish response.

"Some men, including myself, are really stubborn and foolish and it takes an intelligent woman like Abigail to avert a war. To save the household..."

"Amen!" Jayce said loudly beside her.

Abigail and the rest of the row chuckled. Her father looked over in their side of the church and out of the blue said, "I see Brother Jayce Morgan agrees with me. Years ago, I also did a foolish thing and he was affected. I am saying publicly that I am sorry, Jayce, and I mean it. I am also sorry to the band for the past few months that I inconvenienced you. You are our church band and you have been doing a great work. I wish you well in your ministry."

"You know," he said, his voice breaking, "I also wish that my girls were here and that I could say sorry to them individually and collectively for being the kind of fool that I was. As I told you, church, the Lord spoke to me this morning. I need to change my ways or like this foolish Nabal, I may just have his ending."

He continued speaking but Jayce and Abigail looked at each other, both of them dumbfounded, but for different reasons.

Tears sprang to Abby's eyes and she blinked them away. She couldn't look at her father one more minute without breaking down.

"Where's the restroom?" she leaned over to Alice and asked huskily. She didn't want to go around the church building wandering aimlessly with tears streaming down her face.

Alice looked at the tears at the corners of her eyes and touched her hand. "I'll show you."

*****

"That was a Pastor Greenwald shocker," Alice said when Abby exited the bathroom after a long bout of crying. Her eyes were red.

"Let's go sit around the porch at the back," Alice suggested. "Your eyes are blood red."

"Thanks," Abigail said hoarsely.

"No problem." Alice sat on a bench in a relaxed pose and Abby sat beside her.

"The sermon hit a nerve. Didn't it?" Alice asked after a long silence.

"Yes, you could say that."

"That took a lot of nerve on his part," Alice said. "He was admitting things that I never expected him to and asking for forgiveness. I admire that. People always talk about forgiving someone, but it's quite another thing if you are the guilty party and ask for it."

"Yup," Abby said, staring out at the manicured back lawn.

"I remember him from years ago," Alice said wistfully. "His daughter Haley was my friend. We used to call ourselves the first ladies of the New Song band. I was with Carson and she was with Jayce... Haley was afraid of him because he was so strict. She was the youngest child, and boy, did she get the brunt of his discipline. I know it is going to make him extremely sad when he finds out she's dead and he didn't get to tell her sorry."

Abby nodded.

"My therapist would tell him to write a letter," Alice said ruefully. "And put it all down on paper and then bury it."

"You needed a therapist?" Abby asked Alice sharply. "Why?"

Alice sighed. "I have an interesting past that I needed to be at peace with."

"But you have been married to Carson for years!" Abigail said. "What kind of past can you have?"

Alice laughed and then she couldn't stop laughing. After a while she wiped her eyes. "Abigail, you are funny. I was away for ten years; I returned to Jamaica two years ago. I haven't always been here and before that, I had a rough time. I just had to go."

"Before that?" Abigail shook her head. "You got married a few months after high school to the grand love of your life and had a baby shortly after that. You were planning to marry him from when you were a tot. At fourteen you even had your dress picked out. You had the perfect life, except that you lived in Norwood, of course."

Alice stiffened and looked at Abigail, a fierce frown marring her brow. "Who are you?"

Abigail groaned. "Would you be satisfied if I said I guessed?"

"No!" Alice said definitely. "Jayce said you knew things, stuff about us..." She looked at Abigail suspiciously. "You tell me yours and I tell you mine."

"What?" Abigail said, feeling cornered.

"Secret," Alice said. "There is a secret, isn't there? You went to high school with us before or something..."

Abby looked around. There was no one hanging around. She twisted her lips. "If I tell you, you can't tell anyone, not even Jayce. Especially Jayce."

Alice quirked her eyebrows. "Wait, is it a crime? Because I don't think I can keep a crime secret again. I did that for many years and it was not pretty."

"You hid a crime secret?" Abigail whispered.

"Yes," Alice said, "my mother asked me to. So if it is a crime don't tell me. I have zero tolerance for that kind of stuff."

"No," Abby shrugged, "actually, I don't think I can keep a crime secret. I went to the police with it and they kicked me out of the station. So technically I did not keep a secret. Though I might have if the person I witnessed doing the crime did not try to kill me."

"Mmm." Alice looked at her sideways. "Sounds like you have one hell of a secret."

Abby chuckled. "We used to eat green plums with pepper under the poui tree at the back of Cedar Hill High. We used to call Mr. Jerges the English teacher, Mr. Jergens, from the lotion. Oh, and I had to help you arrange your charity concert in order for you to go to the Pantomime in Kingston. That was fun."

Alice shook her head. "I did those things with Haley Greenwald."

"I know," Abigail said. "Remember that night after one of the band concerts when Aaron begged us to break up with Keisha for him?"

Alice squealed and then clamped her hand over her mouth and moved up higher on the bench and away from Abigail. She had shock stamped all over her features and she was actually trembling.

"You two," Jayce said, coming around the corner with a look of concern on his face. "The service is almost done; I thought something was wrong."

Abby looked at Alice fearfully. She was still staring at her as if she had seen a ghost.

Jayce looked between them. "Okay. What's going on?"

"I…er…" Alice cleared her throat. "Abigail says the darndest things." She got up. "She is scandalous, I tell you."

She then turned to look at Abigail again. "We have to pick this up later. You have to call me tonight. No, I'll call you."

Abby nodded, already regretting that she said anything, especially after Jayce looked at Alice's retreating back and then at her with curiosity stamped on his face.

Chapter Seventeen

Abigail tossed and turned the night after the service. She had to hand it to Alice; she had not betrayed any emotions when they met again for the dinner in Aaron's stunning backyard. She had acted normally, laughing and chatting with Abby. She was good, extremely good, but Abby was still worried. She shouldn't have told her anything. What if Alice told Carson? Then Carson told Ian or Xavier. Xavier told Farrah. Farrah told Alka, her best friend. Alka told Aaron and Aaron told Logan. Logan would tell Melody and then, Melody would tell Jayce, for sure, if one of his friends didn't tell him first.

She wouldn't have told Alice if she hadn't broken down like a ninny and cried when she heard her father admitting that he wasn't a good father to his girls and going as far as to apologize to the band and commend their ministry.

His strange humble attitude had been the topic of conversation for most of the evening, with everyone having various theories. Logan had suggested that maybe he was dying.

Jayce thought that maybe he found out that Haley had died. Ian had thought that he was finally converted. "A man could preach and be in the ministry for years and not be converted," he had said.

She liked that theory. It summed up her father well and now it seemed as if he was having a closer look at himself and not liking what he was seeing. Besides, she hated the thought of him dying; in all her years of estrangement from her father and mother, she had always imagined them still strong and healthy.

She didn't want them dead. She wanted them around; she had always had a fantasy of meeting them face-to-face and proving to them that she had done well for herself without them. That had obsessed her for years, especially when she lived with Oliver Hillman. She had wanted to flaunt her wealth in front of them. Luckily, she hadn't done so, but it was tempting.

She got up. Tomorrow was Christmas Eve, and the apartment building was busy with car doors slamming and people shouting. The people to the right of her were watching a comedy, had the television turned up high, and were laughing sporadically.

She gave up trying to sleep. She glanced at the clock. *Eleven o'clock.* She couldn't sleep anyway, with her mind looping like the Jingle Bell record her neighbor to the left was playing. If she heard the song one more time she felt as if she would explode.

She wondered what Jayce was doing. She picked up the phone, itching to call him and then pulled on her black leggings and a racer-back blouse and started pacing. Exercise would help her to go to bed. It wasn't working, though, and after pacing for a short while she was feeling more awake than ever.

She succumbed to calling Jayce. The phone rang twice and he answered sleepily.

"I can't sleep. What are you doing?"

Jayce laughed. "I had my eyes closed and my head on my pillow and..."

"You were sleeping." Abby sighed. "I am so selfish to wake you up."

"I don't mind," Jayce said. "Why can't you sleep?"

"It's noisy over here," Abby said, "and I was thinking. I can't turn my brain off."

"Want to come over?" Jayce asked. "I have three empty rooms."

Abigail paused. "I'll take you up on that. Thanks."

"See you in a while," Jayce said. "Pack for dinner tomorrow and the day after. My friends are trying to outdo each other this year in the entertainment stakes. As the only single member of a coupled-up group, I have loads of invites."

*****

Jayce pulled up at Alice's door twelve minutes later. He hadn't stopped smiling since she called. It gave him a warm melting feeling inside to know that she was lonely and she thought of him. She was serious about him and she didn't know it yet. It was only a matter of time.

He felt a rush of love explode in his chest when she opened her door, the dim light on the outside of her apartment highlighting her toned arms. She had a bag in her hand that looked fairly packed. She was going to spend the Christmas with him. This would be the best Christmas holiday he would celebrate in recent memory.

He finally had an honest-to-goodness girlfriend. Someone he genuinely loved. It made the engagement ring that he had purchased yesterday not seem like a stupid impulse purchase. She gave him hope that he wasn't acting foolishly because even though she said that she didn't like the holidays, she was spending them with him.

When she got in the car she looked at him apologetically. "Sorry to take you out of bed. I just can't take this apartment anymore. I need to find another place to live."

Jayce grinned. "And beyond all of that, you like spending time with me."

"And I like spending time with you," Abby said dutifully.

"Say it like you mean it," Jayce said huskily.

"I mean it," Abby said seriously. She looked at him longingly and then looked away.

Jayce clenched his hand on the steering wheel and then turned on the radio. All of a sudden the sexual tension in the car had heightened, screaming to almost unbearable levels. It didn't help that the songs playing were some of Beres Hammond's classics.

When *No Disturb Sign* came on, Abby shook her head and Jayce cleared his throat. They listened to the music in silence as they headed to his place.

When they reached the house, Jayce murmured, "You can choose any room to sleep in. Mi casa es su casa."

Abby nodded. "Thanks. After that song, I think I'll take the room that's farthest from yours."

Jayce didn't even crack a smile. "That would be a good idea."

Abby headed up the stairs and looked back at Jayce, who was looking at her contemplatively.

"I think we should get married," he said solemnly. He hadn't moved from the door. "I mean, I love you; you must know that. I am not getting any younger, and we have done the requisite cat and mouse dating game thing."

Abigail stopped walking and sat down on the top step of the stairs, stunned.

Jayce slowly walked up to her and sat a step below her. "How do you feel about me...us?"

"What?" Abigail's throat welled up. "Jayce, I love you but I am not who you think I am."

Jayce's heart gave a joyous leap but he shook his head earnestly. "Yes, I know, you have secrets. You were married to an older guy, you divorced, you were burned by this divorce, and you are afraid to get married again. These things happen; it's not that big a deal, Abby."

He moved one step up and sat beside her. "I can deal with that."

Abigail swallowed. "Jayce, I can't marry you without getting you involved in my mess. My nemesis is still alive." She sighed and put her forehead on his. "I am unavailable until then."

Jayce cupped her chin. "Make me understand, Abby. Just tell me whatever it is and we will fight it together."

"No," Abby whispered. "It's a bit more complicated than that and I refuse to get you involved."

"If you would just listen to me," Jayce said softly. "I want to help. Give me a chance to help you through whatever this is. If it's security, we can arrange it, Abby. What has you so scared?"

"I told you already. My ex-husband wants me dead." Abby swallowed. "I saw something I shouldn't have seen and he believes I am dead. If he knows where I am, I will be in trouble."

"Who is your ex-husband?" Jayce asked.

"I can't tell you," Abby said wearily. "I won't tell you."

Jayce groaned. "I am operating in the dark here, Abby. Cut me some slack."

Abby closed her eyes. "I can't. Not now. I am going to bed."

Jayce stood up. "Good night."

He watched as she walked to the guest room farthest from his and closed the door. He couldn't sleep now.

"Thanks, Abby," he whispered resentfully.

He wandered down to his office. He almost snagged his leg on a box he had left in the corner. It was his Haley box; he had been moving it from room to room, not able to make his mind up about throwing away the contents.

It had a huge chunk of his past in there. Why should he throw it away, anyway? Maybe this was the only piece of Haley that was out there in the world. He had been meaning to ask Hillman about her.

He had been meaning to ask Greenwald if he knew that she was dead. He hadn't gotten the chance to question either of the men.

He found a pocketknife in his desk drawer and cut the box open, and the first thing he saw was a stack of letters neatly packed on the top.

He hadn't opened the box in years. In fact, he couldn't remember packing the thing.

He smiled at a caricature that Haley had drawn of him. It wasn't bad. He pulled it out. Maybe he should frame it, keep it in his study. He looked at the little signature at the bottom, Haley G.

He pulled out a stack of CDs. On top was the Maxi Priest CD with Haley's picture on the front. He remembered when she had given it to him the last night that he had seen her, the night that Greenwald had unceremoniously kicked him out of the house.

He studied it intently. She had been such a pretty girl, with a zest for life. Even in the picture there was a sparkle in her eye. Nostalgia rolled over him in waves. By the time he was through with the box he had gone through many memories.

He held a seashell that they picked up at the beach. It was perfectly shaped, with a porcelain sheen, and was pink on the inside.

Haley had joked, "Whenever you say my name in this, I will appear like a genie. I will never leave you, Jay. I will always find you."

Jayce smiled and whispered her name in the shell. They were so childish then. He wondered if they hadn't parted if they would still be together. Carson and Alice were still together and they had known each other longer than he knew Haley. They could have made it work.

But they hadn't and he knew why he was in the box, stirring up the past, rummaging around in the stuff of his youth and mourning once more over Haley. He didn't want to think about Abigail's rejection. He had a sinking feeling that they would not end up together. Abigail seemed determined not to get married, and he was not in the frame of mind to sit around and wait on her while she sorted out her secrets by herself.

So instead of dealing with the here and now and the woman upstairs, he felt like delving a little in familiar heartache ground. Except now he wasn't feeling a heartache; he was feeling a dull pain of regret.

He sighed and pulled the elastic that bound the letters together. Back in the day, he and Haley would write each other letters. They started doing so after a year of knowing each other.

He opened the first letter; he had arranged them according to date. About six or so years ago when he had moved out of his Dad's place and into his first apartment he had found himself reading the letters over again and he may have shed a tear or two. That's when he had put them away.

He looked at the letter now. Haley had taken pride in writing in cursive. She gave her letters elegant loops and under curves and over curves. She loved to write with very fine point pens. Her letters were like a work of art. He read it:

October 5, 1995
Hey Jayce,

Today is our mutual birthday and I am so happy you were born. At least you make my life bearable. I definitely think you are superstitious about bad things happening on your birthday because hey, I am not a bad thing and I happened on your birthday. As you said, you had the day first. Happy Birthday. Live long and prosper. I can't believe you have me hooked on *Star Trek*.

November 3, 1995

Jayce Aman Morgan,

Your name stands for Jam and my mother is making some. I wish you could come over but Daddy said the only XY chromosome that should darken his door is his. He is even talking Biology at the dinner table. It's creepy.

Oh by the way, you won't believe this but I have the lyrics to Water Runs Dry. I listened to it repeatedly. I think I have it perfect this time. It is actually: *Let's don't wait till the water runs dry; we might watch our whole lives pass us by...*

It is not as Carson said, we might watch as the cars pass

us by...

I swear Carson has cars on his brain and that cars thing didn't make sense anyway.

Love you loads.

Haley

Jayce skipped through until he came to the last letter, the one that had given him hope well past the time that it should have. It was at the back of the CD case that she had given him as a going away to school present.

January 7, 1997

Hey Jay, it's Hay.

I was thinking about you last night. Actually, I think about you every night but last night I thought that I feel as if I am going to love you forever. Maybe it's the song on the CD, I don't know. I kind of understand your obsession with it, but I got nostalgic. I just know that this is not just young love, as your father calls it, or some kind of fleeting emotion that teenagers go through.

I know that what I feel for you is the forever kind of feeling, I can imagine myself sitting on some porch somewhere in the future, way in the future—just you and me rocking under the stars and me holding your hand; it's all wrinkly but I don't mind and I say to you, *Jayce we came through all right,* and you nod and say, *Yes Haley, we made it.*

Anyway, as you can see I deliberately wrote this letter

nicely, because I don't want you to lose it. I want you to read it to me on our fiftieth wedding anniversary or something, where all the kids can hear it. It is like a time capsule kind of thing.

I was thinking three kids, tops... or four: two boys and two girls. We'll raise them the best way we know how and hope that they find life-long partners like the both of us.

There I am rambling again...

I feel as if I am going to miss you more than ever this semester when you go away for school, like a rip your heart out kind of missing. I won't eat a morsel of chocolate until I see your face again. I deserve to suffer.

I'll love you for always, Jayce. Never forget it. For always... I'll never stop.

Your Love For Life,
Haley

Jayce clutched the letter to his chest. This was the kind of thing that had him in limbo for years. He closed his eyes. He shouldn't have read it just now. It just confirmed how fickle women were and that *I love you's* were not to be trusted: his mother's, Haley's, or Abigail's.

Chapter Eighteen

Jayce's phone woke him up. It felt as if he had barely gotten into bed. He squinted and looked at the clock. It was six o'clock in the morning on a Christmas Eve, not a workday. He looked on the phone. It was his father.

"Dad," Jayce cleared his throat, "I am not exercising today. I deserve a lie-in."

The General sounded wide-awake and brisk. "Listen, son. We have a little problem. Oliver Hillman is dead; our guy on the early shift found him in bed this morning. We need to check the security footage for any foul play."

Jayce got up swiftly. "Okay. I can access the data feed from my home computer."

He groggily pulled on his robe. He felt a niggling feeling of regret; he wanted to talk to Oliver Hillman about Haley. Now it was too late.

He went to his office and switched on the light. The air was nippy at this time of the morning. He turned on his monitors and typed in the code to access the data feed for Oliver Hillman's residence; the video signal was crystal clear.

He fell asleep in his sofa at eight, with the television watching him. He had a bad bout of coughing at eight-thirty. After that he took a whole bottle of pills. Jayce zoomed into the pill bottle and paused it. Hillman took at least twenty pills with a full bottle of whisky and then he stumbled to bed, coughing again.

There was no movement in the house until the personal security that Oliver had requested to wake him up at five in the morning knocked on his door. Not getting any response, the security pushed the door, went in, and decided to shake him awake.

Hillman killed himself. Jayce sighed. *He was sick and he took a whole bottle of pills, one by one. He probably didn't want to live anymore; he was old and alone, the closest people to him gone. What a sad way to go.*

Jayce flicked off the monitors and called his father. "Dad, it was not foul play. I don't know what pills Hillman took but he took a lot of them."

"Okay," his father said. "Thanks. What are you doing later?"

"Lunch at Logan's, dinner at Ian's. What are you doing?"

"I am going over to Rashida's house."

"What?" Jayce sputtered.

"Apparently Rashida was not after me," The General chuckled. "She was trying to set me up with her mother, who is age-appropriate and very much my type of woman: relaxed, friendly, mature, outspoken and caring.

"I only realized that after she dragged her poor mother to the office last week under false pretenses. I thought she had invited me to lunch and I went down to the cafeteria to tell her that she was too young for me and all that but she introduced me to her mom and disappeared, then we got to talking."

Jayce exhaled fully. "Thank God. I would have to commit you to hospital if you ended up with Rashida."

"She might become your stepsister." The General cleared his throat. "We will see how it goes."

Jayce laughed. "Okay, sir. Have a good day. You know you deserve some happiness."

"And you too," his father said gruffly. "What is Abigail doing for Christmas?"

"Whatever I am doing," Jayce said, sobering up. "She is staying over here. I proposed last night and she turned me down."

"Is she crazy?" his father asked indignantly. "You are the best thing to ever happen to her."

"Only you Dad, my cheering squad of one." Jayce laughed, "I am not giving up, I might be able to convince her yet."

"You do that." His father hung up the phone.

Jayce went to the kitchen and put on the kettle. Outside, it was still dark; the sky was taking its time to brighten up. He put a tea bag into one of the cups and swirled it while absentmindedly thinking about Haley and Oliver Hillman and Abigail and her husband. The similarities with the situations couldn't be missed. Haley had married an older guy who Abigail had suggested might have killed her, though he didn't believe that theory. Why would Hillman even want to do that?

Abigail was paranoid because her ex-husband was out to get her. If only she would tell him what his name was. Then he could do so many things to help. He knew the right law enforcement channels to tap. That was what he and his father did for a living. Abigail was making a big mistake in not telling him.

He carried his tea to his desk and brought up the file with her name. He had slowly been gathering information on her. She had given him no choice since she wouldn't tell him about her past.

He glanced at the bare data that he had on her; it was as if her life started a year and a half ago. Then it clicked. Maybe Abigail was not even her right name. What type of ninny was he? All this time the clues were there: there was no data on her birth date, or high school, or parents.

He put the cup down on his desk abruptly, sloshing some of the liquid on the side. Why hadn't he thought of that before? He opened the desk drawer. He always kept a pack of tissue in there. He rummaged around, hoping to find a pack before the water spread toward his keyboard.

Then his hand hit some papers: the lists that Abigail had made for the furnishing. He had barely glanced at them at the time. He took them out; they would have to do and besides, he didn't need them again.

He placed the first one down on the water and it quickly absorbed the wetness, creating an even bigger mess. He got up to get napkins this time, but the writing on the top list got his attention. It was in cursive. The loops and the swirls were so familiar; he had just seen them late last night in Haley's box. He sat down abruptly, again a breathless feeling of disbelief overtaking him.

"No," he whispered. His chest constricted and he was finding it difficult to breathe.

He closed his eyes. The first time he met Abigail Petri, it was as if a shaft of lightning had hit him. It was a Thursday. He could see it in his mind's eye. He had gone to Searock and headed to the VIP section upstairs as usual, where the place was air- conditioned. He hated to eat in the hustle and bustle of downstairs; he liked to look out on the view while he savored the food.

It was a year and seven months ago. Abigail had stopped when she saw him. She had been coming up the stairs and she literally stopped. She had been checking him out. He hadn't made up that scene in his mind. He had subsequently excused it because he thought that no woman had ever stopped when they saw him because they found him attractive.

Then she had walked over to him with a wide smile on her face, as if she knew him, as if she was happy to see him. He had responded to that smile. He had responded to her as if he had known her.

He didn't know how, he didn't know why, he didn't even know if it were true, but he would bet the very house that he was sitting in that Abigail Petri was Haley Greenwald.

He felt dizzy for a moment, just absorbing the facts. She knew his friends because they had been her friends too. The picture on the kitchen wall she knew the year of, even though there was no year on it, was because she had taken that picture. She loved raisins in her porridge. She knew most of his likes and dislikes without him telling her. She had been married to an old guy who wanted her dead and when she saw Oliver Hillman she had an unusual panic attack. The thought made him sit up. Oliver Hillman was now dead. What would she do now?

He wanted to go and confront her and find out her story, but he was going to play this smart. He shook his head in disbelief. What if he were wrong? The coincidences were too many to be ignored, and handwriting rarely lies.

Chapter Nineteen

Abigail woke up to the sound of whistling. She had no idea that after that intense conversation with Jayce last night she would have fallen asleep, but she went out like a light as soon as her head touched the pillow. Maybe that was what she needed, a different bed. She showered quickly and pulled on her red maxi dress. It seemed appropriate for the season and she had packed it with that in mind.

She looked at the clock. It was nine o'clock. Jayce must have been up for a while. He was in the backyard watering the plants and whistling.

"Hey," she called to him, opening the patio doors and looking out.

"Hey." Jayce gave her an intense look and then came over to her. He put down the can and grabbed her in a bear hug. He squeezed her so tight, Abby had to protest. "What are you doing?"

"I am happy to see you." Jayce raked his eyes over her

face.

"Okay," Abigail said, grinning, "I am happy to see you too. You look happy."

"I am happy. I love you." Jayce kissed her hard.

"Wow," Abby grinned back. "I love you too."

"And you are going to marry me," Jayce continued.

"Didn't you hear what I said last night?" Abby drew back from Jayce.

Jayce nodded. "Yup, but I don't care."

"Jayce..." Abby said fearfully.

"Stop trying to protect me," Jayce said harshly. "You know, when all of this is over, I have a cussing for you."

"All of what is over?" Abby looked at him strangely. "What has gotten into you?"

The doorbell rang and he looked at her fiercely. "I invited Pastor Greenwald and Sister Greenwald over this morning."

"You did?" Abigail opened her eyes wide. "Why?"

"Because they are a part of my closure." Jayce headed to the door. "Remember, I was grieving over my ex-girlfriend. Last night I read one of her letters and I realized that I am not really over her. Maybe I'll never be over her," Jayce said over his shoulders.

Abigail pressed her lips together. They were trembling. What was Jayce saying? She heard her father's deep voice in the foyer and she headed upstairs.

"No, you aren't going anywhere." Jayce looked at Abigail severely. "You are going to stay for this."

"No, I am not," Abigail said, petrified to see her parents face-to-face and bewildered at Jayce for pushing Haley in her face so strongly this morning.

"Come on," Jayce said sternly. "You will want to hear this. The pastor is going to confess something about Haley."

"He is?" Abigail turned around and headed down the stairs,

curiosity getting the best of her.

"Funny, isn't it?" Jayce asked her. "How you like hearing about Haley."

"Well, she sounds like an interesting girl," Abigail said uncomfortably. "You certainly think so. I am interested in what you are interested in."

Jayce chuckled.

They entered the living room. Pastor Greenwald was studying a picture...

It was the picture of them, the old picture of the band with her and Alice and Keisha: the ladies of the New Song band. She hadn't seen it before. Jayce must have found it last night.

Pastor Greenwald turned around. "I didn't know you had company."

Abigail almost missed what Jayce said because she was looking at her mother. She was seated in the settee with a sketch in her hand.

Abigail was torn between looking at what the sketch depicted and drinking in her mother. Fourteen years. She hadn't aged much, except for a sprinkling of gray hairs where there had been black and a slight sag to her jaw. She was aging well and looked remarkably composed. She looked a bit like an older version of Beatrice, Abby realized.

She snapped her head around when Pastor Greenwald held out his hand to her. She put hers in his and shook it. She didn't hear Jayce's explanation of why she was there. Sis Greenwald looked up at her and smiled sweetly, with a twinkle in her eye.

"My Haley drew this," she said, holding up the picture.

Abigail sat down across from her and saw that it was a sketch she had done of her family. She had dreams of being an artist a long time ago. Jayce sat down beside her, and Pastor Greenwald remained standing.

"You said you had news about Haley?" he asked, an anxious note to his voice.

"Yes," Jayce said. "I found out that she died four years ago."

"No." Her mother's eyes were the first to well up with tears and then her father walked stiltedly to the living room window, keeping his back to them.

"What killed her?" he asked hoarsely.

"Car accident," Jayce said, "but I have to admit it's strange. There is no record of a burial or even where her grave is, but there's a death certificate."

Her mother started sobbing in earnest and Abigail wanted to shout at Jayce to stop. How could he be so cruel in telling about Haley's death so abruptly and unsympathetically? She realized when she saw the very real grief of the people in front of her that they weren't as indifferent to her as she had thought.

"I caused it." Pastor Greenwald turned around. His eyes were red and damp. "My family is in a shambles, Jayce, and I caused it."

Jayce nodded and glanced at Abigail. She had tears in her eyes as well, and she didn't even realize.

"I beat her so badly that night when you came over to the house that my wife thought she was dead the morning after." He shook his head, "I was so ashamed of what I did after I did it that I couldn't face her the day after. I was happy that she went away, so I wouldn't have to admit how much I was wrong. I was beating her but in reality I was beating myself."

He swallowed and said gruffly, "You might as well know. We conceived our first girl out of wedlock. I was going to theological school but I was wild. Hannah was one of six girls I was seeing, and she was the one who got pregnant."

He reached in his pocket and found a kerchief. "I had to

marry her and put a good spin on it. You know, re-invent myself as a strait-laced kind of guy."

"So you were extremely hard on your girls because of that?" Jayce responded with a sigh.

"Yes," Pastor Greenwald nodded, "but ironically I drove them straight into harm. Haley was our last chance to get things right. Hannah had difficulty with her pregnancy and we knew we couldn't have any more children. I was determined that the last one would be perfect."

"He changed when we got married," Hannah whispered. "He became someone I didn't like."

"But I am doing better," Greenwald said to Hannah.

"Yes," Hannah nodded. "You are."

"So why didn't you contact your daughter after she left?" Abigail demanded. "Why show grief now, when you had years and years to get in touch with her?"

Her eyes swiveled between them.

Pastor Greenwald looked like he was about to protest at her, a stranger, questioning them but he said instead, "It was shame. I forbade Hannah to contact her. I didn't want to face what I had done. I didn't want to say I was sorry and beg her to come back home."

Abigail got up.

"Where are you going?" Jayce asked.

"I don't want to hear any more," Abigail said, moving toward the door.

"But why?" Jayce asked. "You don't know Haley; this shouldn't affect you in any way at all."

Abby stopped. She really was acting weird for somebody who was not supposed to know these people. She couldn't turn around, though. For the life of her, she couldn't stand to see their grief for Haley. She wanted to yell at them and contrarily she wanted to hug them.

They were as flawed as everybody else and they had really bungled the whole parenting thing, both of them. Instead of being himself, her father had allowed the guilt of his past to turn him into a fire-spitting monster who was determined to correct his mistakes by punishing his children for what he imagined were his traits. In his eagerness to do so, he had watched as each of his girls fell into the same pit that he did.

Burdened with guilt because of how they had started out, her mother had turned into a mouse, not wanting to deal with her past.

Abigail breathed out. She wanted to start over with them—she was tired of being somebody else—but she couldn't. She took two steps to the door.

"He is dead, Abby," Jayce said quietly. "He died this morning...took twenty-odd pills with a whole bottle of whisky."

Abigail stiffened. She felt as if she literally couldn't move. "Who is dead?"

She slowly turned around. The Greenwalds were watching their exchange curiously and Jayce was looking at her with sympathy in his eyes.

"Oliver Hillman." He reeled the name off smoothly.

Abigail swayed where she was. Why was he telling her that? Did he know who she really was?

"Yes," Jayce said in reply to her unspoken question. "I know."

Abigail sank to the floor. She didn't faint; she just sat where she was. Her mind felt locked and frozen.

"Is she all right?" Hannah was looking at her with concern.

"Yes, she is," Jayce said, "more than all right. She is just in shock. That's all."

He looked at the Greenwalds. "This will come as a shock to you, as it did me, but this is Haley. She had to reinvent herself because she feared for her life. I am sure she will tell you the story later, because I am also sure that she wants to reconcile with you."

Greenwald gasped. "What?"

*****

It took them a further half an hour to leave; Hannah clung to Abby, hugging her as they cried together. Jayce had to cancel lunch with Logan.

"But why?" Melody asked. "We can't have lunch without you."

She had barely accepted his excuses when Jayce hung up the phone.

"Haley," he whispered. She was catatonic on the couch. "Should I call you Haley or Abby?"

Fresh tears sprang to Abby's eyes. "I like both names. It is going to feel strange to be Haley again. I will be Haley with a different face. I can't believe that you know. How?"

"Your handwriting." Jayce hunkered beside her. "All this time, my heart knew but it took the rest of me time to catch up. Last night I was reading one of your letters from '97 and I compared it to a list that you did the other day. It clicked... then everything clicked."

"Listen," he looked into her tear-washed eyes, "I am not into long engagements. I am not letting you out of my sight again for the foreseeable future and I just want you to know that I loved you then, and I love you now, whoever you are and however you look."

Haley grinned and pulled him down to her. "I love you too, Jayce, forever and always."

October 5, 2012

They were in the warehouse again, upstairs in the band room. This time all of them had a wife by their side. The couple of the hour was Jayce and Haley. The banners read 'Happy Birthday Jay and Hay'. They were all dressed in white because General Morgan had decided that today was as good a day as any to get married and he wanted a white wedding. They had just returned from his reception at the beach.

"I had to throw a party today," Melody said, on the mike, "because this day is a glorious day for us. It is our friends' birthday, Jayce and Haley."

She cleared her throat. "Xavier and Farrah have a little announcement to make and my hubby was promoted to senior partner in his law firm today. Let's just say, for the record, that Jayce's curse theory has failed. This day is splendiferous. I don't know if that's a word and I don't care." She laughed and did a little jig.

Jayce laughed. He was sitting in his favorite beanbag chair but this time, he had company. Haley was snuggled in his lap. So much had happened in the past year that he was thinking that his blessing cup was overflowing. They too had a little announcement to make; they had only found out this morning that Haley was expecting.

The Greenwalds were constant visitors to the house now, and as Haley liked to remark, her father's transformation was a miracle. Pastor Greenwald had gone humble. When Jayce teased him about it, he always remarked that he was in a better place now. It was better to be humble and admit you are wrong than to be full of pride without a family around. His other girls had slowly started visiting again after Haley had tentatively extended a hand of friendship to them. Their reaction was encouraging. It was as if they had been waiting to come home.

They still had their kinks and their differences of opinion. Just last week, Haley and her father had a showdown about his attitude. It had ended well, with Greenwald actually saying sorry.

Melody jolted him from his reminiscing, saying, "The band will now, as a yearly favor to Jayce, play his favorite song. *Ain't It Enough* by Maxi Priest."

Jayce grinned. "Thanks guys!"

"You should be thankful," Carson mumbled. "I can't understand why you like this song so much, though. Never could, and let it be known that I will complain every year until you find a new favorite song."

"It's simple," Jayce laughed, "a girl named Haley wrote me a letter and put it at the back of the CD with this particular song, and she told me that she would love me forever and always. The letter and the song became synonymous to me. See: mystery solved."

Carson grinned. "Got it. And we all know you will never get over this Haley girl."

"Nope, never," Jayce said. "Never ever." He kissed her softly as the opening notes to the song swelled around them.

The End

Keep reading for an excerpt from **Perfect Melody**

Logan and Melody's story

Melody straightened her spine and viewed herself in the mirror. She looked like a cross between a warrior princess and a harem belly dancer. Dramatic makeup highlighted her chestnut brown eyes; what she thought were short eyelashes were now long and lush after she applied mascara. Her skin was smooth and unblemished, thanks to the wonders of the right foundation. Her full lips were practically sparkling with a tan lipstick called Fairy Dust.

Her clothes were also perfectly chosen to give the impression of a femme fatale on the prowl. Her red dress was accentuated with sparkly dust; its sleeves flared. The dress bared her smooth midsection, which didn't look too bad after the twins. Her matching red stilettos, which she had long kicked off, were in the corner of the room. She contemplated going for them but felt it was too much trouble.

Instead, she positioned the camera toward the bed, which was littered in red roses, posed in the center of the shot, and tried to look seductive. She twisted and preened as she pressed the timer on the camera, over and over. As the flash went off she dared various positions and then finally she got tired. *That would have to do.*

She hung off the edge of the bed, not wanting her foundation to mess up the ivory sheets. One by one the tears gathered, especially when she heard the clock in the living room chime just once. It was one in the morning—an unholy time to be awake and alone on your anniversary and taking pointless pictures to memorialize it.

She had put on the dress and makeup six hours ago and felt like a princess. She had straightened her naturally curly hair so it would flow to her waist and had even put on a red diamond studded tiara. She had a fantasy that she would be the harem girl and Logan would be king. They sometimes role-played to spice up their sex life, and weeks ago at breakfast Logan had suggested that he had an Eastern fantasy and winked at her.

She had liked the idea, and when she liked something she usually went all out with it. She had gone so far as to have the outfits made and had fixed the interior of the room like a tent; sheer jewel-like material draped the king sized bed, approximating what she imagined an exotic Arabian tent would look like. She had spent most of the day preparing the room. She had even sent the children to Alice and Carson, relieved that they were not underfoot while she worked steadily.

When she viewed herself in the mirror with the decorative backdrop, after her exhaustive day of renovating, she had liked what she was seeing. She had really captured the fantasy.

Today she didn't look like Zack and Lauren's mother, or president of the PTA, or Sis Melody, head of the church's welfare department, nor did she look like the manager of the New Song Band. She had felt dominant, passionate, and alluring and she had looked it. Her background Arabic music had even complemented the room. She was in full seductive mood; even her perfume wafting up to her nose was a turn-on. Her stilettos made her feel tall and in charge.

But now, slumped on the bed, she felt the vestiges of depression creeping upon her. For the past few months she had tried to stop the depression, but since her initial happiness at Logan's promotion she had realized that she had nothing much to celebrate. They had more money than ever, and it was Logan's dream come true to make senior partner, but in just four short months she was starting to realize the huge toll his promotion was having on all aspects of his life.

He had run out of their Christmas celebrations because of some new finding on his case and New Year celebrations were a nonstarter with him on the phone with other managing partners discussing business. These days he hardly had time for band practice; sometimes he would even forget that it was Wednesday. And now the biggest blunder of them all, the ultimate insult to injury: Logan forgot one of their key anniversaries, the one that he had insisted that they celebrate or it would be a clear sign that their romance was dying.

They had three anniversaries as opposed to the one that normal couples had. They celebrated the day they met, which was pretty dramatic; he had saved her from drowning at the beach, ten years ago today.

Their next yearly celebration was the day they fell in love, which took place on March 1, and their third anniversary was the day they married, which was in June.

It was cute and sappy and their friends thought it ridiculous but Logan had insisted that he always wanted to remember the day that he saved her and to commemorate it they had to have a yearly anniversary, where they had no kids around, no friends around—just them and whichever fantasy they had managed to envision for the day, and through the years they had really come up with some zingers.

It would be surprising to many persons, even his closest friends, that Logan, universally known as serious and firm and self-possessed, could be romantic and generous and given to over-the-top gestures.

He hadn't even called today. She had until now thought that he would have come home and surprised her earlier in the evening; some years he pretended to forget and then had the most wonderful surprises after his 'forgetfulness', but these days she could sense that Logan was not all here and it bothered her.

She refused to call him; he would answer the phone and sound distant and possibly snap at her as he did yesterday, and she didn't know if she could take an abrupt stilted conversation right now. She felt like an idiot for preparing for this night so thoroughly. She sniffed and grabbed a wad of tissues from the drawer at the side of the bed.

*****

Logan glanced at the time and raked his hand through his hair. Where had the time gone? He had not even dented the trial brief that he had to present tomorrow in court. He was covered in paperwork, trying to acquaint himself with a case that he had inherited from Thaddeus Masters the third, founding partner of Masters, Gilrich and Edison.

He had been offered the incredible position of managing partner and he had grabbed it with both arms.

Managing partners got a higher percentage of the profits; they chose cases, voted on important company decisions and in general had more free time. What he was doing now was grunt work, and not even work in his area. Thaddeus Masters had personally asked him, with the suspicion of tears in his eyes, to deal with this case for him.

That alone had intrigued Logan. Thaddeus was as tough as nails and as shrewd as an old fox but this case involved his illegitimate daughter, a spa employee who had accidentally killed her client in a bizarre set of circumstances that he, as her reluctant lawyer, was still trying to figure out.

Logan should have said no to taking the case. He was not acquainted with the ins and outs of criminal law. He was a Family Lawyer and was more comfortable in family court. Give him a regular old divorce case any day, or a child support or spousal support situation and he would feel at home, but this was a pain. Thaddeus owed him big time because he knew he could not help out his secret daughter without being exposed. Thaddeus had to confide in him.

Logan grabbed the stack of papers in front of him that had been prepared by his legal secretary, Sabrina, and Thaddeus' own paralegal, Kendra, who was assigned to help him with this case.

"Where are the Costner files?" Logan searched through the tall stack of papers on his desk. "I can't find them."

"They are right here, Mr. Moore." Sabrina placed them on his desk and said sleepily, "You look like you need a break."

"I do." Logan looked at the clock and said crisply, "But if I make it through the night, do this brief, I am going to run home get a shave and shower and head to court. Tomorrow is my anniversary, so after court I am taking the day off."

Sabrina lost her sleepy look instantly when he spoke of his anniversary. She had been working with him for six months now and she had silently gathered data on him and his wife Melody. Some of it was a part of her job; the rest was just a hobby.

"You know, I thought your anniversary was today. You have three of them on your calendar. Today, or should I say yesterday since it's after one in the morning, was one of them."

Logan looked up at her. Even in his tired state and with slightly blood shot eyes he was handsome. Sabrina prepared herself for the familiar thrill of staring at him and was not disappointed. She had grown quite adept at hiding her complete adoration for him but in situations like this when they were working late, his tie all askew, his eyes looking sleepy, she had the insane urge to declare her feelings for him and beg him to love her back.

He groaned and slapped his hand on his head. "Melody is going to kill me. You are looking at a dead man."

Sabrina shook her head slightly and thought, *No, she*

wouldn't kill you. No woman in her right mind would think of killing a fine specimen such as you. ...

OTHER BOOKS BY BRENDA BARRETT

Love Triangle Series

Love Triangle: Three Sides To The Story- George, the husband, Marie, the wife and Karen-the mistress. They all get to tell their side of the story.

Love Triangle: After The End--Torn between two lovers. Colleen married her high school sweetheart, Isaiah, hoping that they would live happily ever after but life intruded and Isaiah disappeared at sea. She found work with the rich and handsome, Enrique Lopez, as a housekeeper and realized that she couldn't keep him at arms length...

Love Triangle: On The Rebound--For Better or Worse, Brandon vowed to stay with Ashley, but when worse got too much he moved out and met Nadine. For the first time in years he felt happy, but then Ashley remembered her wedding vows...

New Song Series

Going Solo (New Song Series-Book 1)- Carson Bell, had a lovely voice, a heart of gold, and was no slouch in the looks department. So why did Alice abandon him and their daughter? What did she want after ten years of silence?

Duet on Fire (New Song Series- Book 2)- Ian and Ruby had problems trying to conceive a child. If that wasn't enough, her ex-lover the current pastor of their church wants her back...

Tangled Chords (New Song Series- Book 3)- Xavier Bell, the poor, ugly duckling has made it rich and his looks have been incredibly improved too. Farrah Knight, hotel heiress had cruelly rejected him in the past but now she needed help. Could Xavier forgive and forget?

Broken Harmony(New Song Series-Book 4)- Aaron Lee, wanted the top job in his family company but he had a moral clause to consider just when Alka, his married ex-girlfriend walks back into his life.

A Past Refrain (New Song Series-Book 5)- Jayce had issues with forgetting Haley Greenwald even though he had a new woman in his life. Will he ever be able to shake his love for Haley?

Perfect Melody (New Song Series- Book 6)- Logan Moore had the perfect wife, Melody but his secretary Sabrina was hell bent on breaking up the family. Sabrina wanted Logan whatever the cost and she had a secret about Melody, that could shatter Melody's image to everyone.

The Bancroft Family Series

Homely Girl (The Bancrofts- Book 0) - April and Taj were opposites in so many ways. He was the cute, athletic boy that everybody wanted to be friends with. She was the overweight, shy, and withdrawn girl. Do April and Taj have a love that can last a lifetime? Or will time and separate paths rip them apart?

Saving Face (The Bancrofts- Book 1) - Mount Faith

University drama begins with a dead president and several suspects including the president in waiting Ryan Bancroft.

Tattered Tiara (The Bancrofts- Book 2) - Micah Bancroft is targeted by femme fatale Deidra Durkheim. There are also several rape cases to be solved.

Private Dancer (The Bancrofts- Book 3) Adrian Bancroft was gutted when he returned to Jamaica and found out that his first and only love Cathy Taylor was a stripper and was literally owned by the menacing drug lord, Nanjo Jones.

Goodbye Lonely (The Bancrofts- Book 4) - Kylie Bancroft was shy and had to resort to going to confidence classes. How could she win the love of Gareth Beecher, her faculty adviser, a man with a jealous ex-wife in his past and a current mystery surrounding a hand found in his garden?

Practice Run (The Bancrofts Book 5) - Marcus Bancroft had many reasons to avoid Mount Faith but Deidra Durkheim was not one of them. Unfortunately, on one of his visits he was the victim of a deliberate hit and run.

Sense of Rumor (The Bancrofts- Book 6) - Arnella Bancroft was the wild, passionate Bancroft, the creative loner who didn't mind living dangerously; but when a terrible thing happened to her at her friend Tracy's party, it changed her. She found that courting rumors can be devastating and that only the truth could set her free.

A Younger Man (The Bancrofts- Book 7)- Pastor Vanley Bancroft loved Anita Parkinson despite their fifteen-year age gap, but Anita had a secret, one that she could not reveal to

Vanley. To tell him would change his feelings toward her, or force him to give up the ministry that he loved so much.

Just To See Her (The Bancrofts- Book 8)- Jessica Bancroft had the opportunity to meet her fantasy guy Khaled, he was finally coming to Mount Faith but she had feelings for Clay Reid, a guy who had all the qualities she was looking for. Who would she choose and what about the weird fascination Khaled had for Clay?

The Three Rivers Series

Private Sins (Three Rivers Series-Book 1)- Kelly, the first lady at Three Rivers Church was pregnant for the first elder of her church. Could she keep the secret from her husband and pretend that all was well?

Loving Mr. Wright (Three Rivers Series- Book 2)- Erica saw one last opportunity to ditch her single life when Caleb Wright appeared in her town. He was perfect for her, but what was he hiding?

Unholy Matrimony (Three Rivers Series- Book 3) - Phoebe had a problem, she was poor and unhappy. Her solution to marry a rich man was derailed along the way with her feelings for Charles Black, the poor guy next door.

If It Ain't Broke (Three Rivers Series- Book 4)- Chris Donahue wanted a place in his child's life. Pinky Black just wanted his love. She also wanted him to forget his obsession with Kelly and love her. That shouldn't be so hard? Should it?

Contemporary Romance/Drama

The Preacher And The Prostitute - Prostitution and the clergy don't mix. Tell that to ex-prostitute, Maribel, who finds herself in love with the Pastor at her church. Can an ex-prostitute and a pastor have a future together?

New Beginnings - Inner city girl Geneva was offered an opportunity of a lifetime when she found out that her 'real' father was a very wealthy man. Her decision to live up-town meant that she had to leave Froggie, her 'ghetto don,' behind. She also found herself battling with her stepmother and battling her emotions for Justin, a suave up-towner.

Full Circle- After graduating from university, Diana wanted to return to Jamaica to find her siblings. What she didn't foresee was that she would meet Robert Cassidy and that both their pasts would be intertwined, and that disturbing questions would pop up about their parentage, just when they were getting close.

Historical Fiction/Romance

The Empty Hammock- Workaholic, Ana Mendez, fell asleep in a hammock and woke up in the year 1494. It was the time of the Tainos, a time when life seemed simpler, but Ana knew that all of that was about to change.

The Pull Of Freedom- Even in bondage the people, freshly arrived from Africa, considered themselves free. Led by Nanny and Cudjoe the slaves escaped the Simmonds' plantation and went in different directions to forge their destiny in the new country called Jamaica.

Jamaican Comedy (Material contains Jamaican dialect)

Di Taxi Ride And Other Stories- Di Taxi Ride and Other Stories is a collection of twelve witty and fast paced short stories. Each story tells of a unique slice of Jamaican life.

CPSIA information can be obtained at www.ICGtesting.com
Printed in the USA
LVOW06s2134260715

447744LV00008B/65/P

9 789768 247186